On Balance

KM Neale

Jess!
Hope you enjoy this!
K.M. Neale
x

CHAPTER 1

Clive Alwynn woke in a cold sweat, sitting bolt upright, breathing hard. 'God,' he whispered. 'God.' He shook off the dream and turned to his wife. She was deep in sleep. He wondered what she dreamed of, as he slid his hand slowly up beneath her t-shirt. She turned away, slightly, her glasses pushed askew, the open book sliding from the bed. Sebastian paced the foot of the bed, purring impatiently, the dog rolled onto her back, legs splayed, growling low. 'Bella!' he reached down to stroke her belly.

He went downstairs, put on the kettle and rattled biscuits into ceramic bowls: DOG. CAT. He showered and dressed, looped his tie into a loose knot, and stared into the mirror. In four hours' time he'd be presenting the highest profile pitch of his career. He'd been with AdVerbe Advertising for three years, and had become one of their most successful, if not most unpredictable, account directors. Today's win would confirm that he was more than just a maverick, more than just another smart-mouthed, over-ambitious sales guy who was good with words.

He'd worked hard for this moment – always at the office, always on the phone, Blackberry always to hand. The strain had killed his first marriage, and he'd realised when he'd married Nic that he'd have to find a balance.

At first it wasn't hard; he could hardly bear to be apart from her – the thrill of rushing home, the unbearable anxiety when traffic delayed him, the slight panic that maybe she wouldn't be there.

But now, nearly two years on, he'd found the security that allowed him to work late knowing she was safely tucked away in the British Library poring over the past. And over the last month, this new pitch for Feldmann's had kept him at the office later and later, but he reassured himself that it was temporary, short-term, and soon he'd have the time she deserved.

Feldmann's was one of Europe's oldest banks. Family-owned, the three brothers had fought off sporadic take-over bids, and now they realised that, if the bank was to survive, it was time to modernise.

This year they would re-launch, offering everything their technologically advanced competitors promised – an incredible leap for the three brothers, the youngest of whom was 66. And for the first time in its history, Feldmann's had decided to harness the power of advertising, rather than relying on the discreet word-of-mouth of the down-at-heel European bourgeoisie.

Clive's challenge was to reassure the brothers that he understood the dynamic of moving forward in an unfamiliar world. He'd met two of the brothers and several Board members and recognised that they were, in fact, deeply afraid of these forced changes. He'd grasped their fear and made it the heart of his campaign: going forward didn't mean leaving the past behind, he'd told the creative team. 'Don't think of 'past' as in baggage,' he'd stressed. 'Past - as in foundations, history... a legacy. A way of going forward.' Two other agencies were pitching for the account. Clive knew, instinctively, that they would frame Feldmann's relaunch as a brave leap forward, a jettisoning of the past.

And he knew in his gut that the brothers Feldmann would reject this approach, even if he didn't fully appreciate why. The past was a strange place to Clive; he had never really understood it, never really considered it. People like his wife seemed to have a need to revisit it, access it – via books and films and the music she listened to. But Clive didn't see the point.

His own past was uneventful enough – birth, Uni, marriage, kids, divorce, love, new wife; like most 47-year-old men. For Clive, time always moved forward – there was always something just around the next corner that could, if he wasn't ready, knock him sideways into a terrible silence, a grey stillness. The past lay like evaporating rain puddles in the road, always receding in the rear-view mirror, never interesting enough and never as powerful as the curve just ahead.

'Nic?' he whispered. 'Tea.' She sighed and stretched beneath the blankets. He straightened her glasses again. He didn't like them; they looked like something an old woman would wear – frameless and always slipping down her nose - but she couldn't be persuaded to buy a new pair. She'd had them for 15 years – bought them when she was studying in the States. Ignoring fashion, ignoring aesthetics and ignoring the fact that sight degenerated over time, she clung to them as though they held every page they'd ever passed over.

She reached out for the cup without opening her eyes. 'What time is it?'

'Just after 6. I'm off.'

'Hey,' she opened her eyes and pushed away her glasses. 'Good luck.'

He grimaced theatrically. 'Yeah.' He leaned forward to kiss the soft frown lines of her forehead. 'See you tonight.'

The traffic into town was already building. He passed the nursery down the hill where he'd often dropped his boys, still sleepy and yawning in the back seat, on his way to another early meeting. An image of Jack and Ben flashed into his mind, an unwelcome snapshot of wild, blond curls, pristine school uniforms, toothy grins. Virginia sent the shots as dutifully as she sent the Father's Day, Christmas and Birthday cards. She'd taken the boys with her when she'd been offered the job in New York two years ago.

It had been, she'd said, an offer she couldn't refuse: Stansons was one of the best magazine publishers in the US, and she was one of the best designers in London.

He hadn't contested her taking the boys. He'd had no idea what to say. It was over; already receding in the rear-view. He'd realised as the cab pulled away into the night that they were gone, and he'd sat in the darkness of the lounge for hours. By morning, there was nothing to do but make coffee, shower and drive out into the day.

A blue BMW cut in front of him, and he slammed on the brakes.

'Fucker!' he shouted, punching at the horn.

Deep breath. He needed to focus on Feldmann's. He wanted this account. Time. Time was nothing, but he had to hold it, had to smell it, appreciate it, hold it up to the light and treat it like the precious creature the Feldmann brothers believed it to be. He knew he'd win. He had to win. He turned up the CD and opened the sunroof to the chilly air, summoning the rush of adrenalin.

He arrived at the office just after 8, and was glad to see most of the team were already there. Mitchell, the designer, leaned back in his seat, studying his computer screen, nodding to the beat in his head phones. His project manager Stephanie was looking harassed and worried, barking orders into the telephone.

'I want them mounted and ready to go now! I don't care if upstairs has snowed you under. Just tell them: there wouldn't be an upstairs if we didn't win any pitches!' And she slammed down the phone, looking up and smiling brightly when she saw Clive. 'Morning!'

Clive smiled. He liked his new team; technically they weren't his – they were part of Palmer's group, and they'd been 'loaned' to him for the pitch. Clive wasn't happy with the situation – Palmer had been poking his nose into the project every chance he had for the last seven weeks, watching the work progress, silently, but waiting for the chance to swoop and claim the account as his own – after the win.

Well, he could go to hell, thought Clive. James McKinnie, the MD, had promised Clive complete control of the account should he win it. And he knew that Palmer's team would love the chance to defect. Palmer's reputation with the junior staff was as bad as it was upstairs.

He sipped his coffee and scanned through the script again.

'Steph?' he called out through his door. 'What time's the...?'

'Taxi at 8.30 – 15 minutes, Clive.'

'Great. Round up the troops will you?'

He thanked the team for all of their hard work and hurried down to the lobby. Marina, the head of Adverbe's corporate account arm was fidgeting with an unlit cigarette and her lighter, and she lit up as soon as the revolving door spilled them out into the street.

'Hey Clive. I went through the figures last night – they look very good, indeed. We could have gone higher, you know.'

Clive laughed. 'That's the default of your department, Marina. No, trust me: we won't be able to pull the wool over this guy's eyes. Feldmann's a canny bugger. He'll appreciate our transparency.'

Marina smiled. 'Yeah, well....' And she exhaled a relaxed cloud of smoke. 'So it's a standard pitch then? You go through the creative, I'll set out the financials?'

'Yes, please. I've got a very brief creative outline – they're more interested in the numbers at this stage.'

The Feldmann's London building was an austere, unobtrusive structure in Portland Place. A young woman welcomed them into the hush of the marbled lobby, and handed them each an ID badge. They followed her to a large office, where four men sat around a polished oak table.

'Mr Alwynn,' Gustav Feldmann rose to his feet and shook Clive's hand. 'Welcome. And Ms Merriland. May I introduce you to my colleagues?'

Introductions over and coffee served, Clive and Marina made their pitch. The hour passed quickly; the Board members had plenty of finance questions, and Clive was glad to have Marina to hand.

It seemed like moments later that they were shaking hands again and being ushered out of the building.

Back at the office, Clive told the team it had gone well... but now they had to wait and see. He was checking his emails when Palmer tapped at his door.

'Ah... Palmer. Come in.'

'So, how did it go?' Palmer fell back into a chair, his small round belly straining at his expensive shirt. 'What's your immediate response? Good? Could do better? I haven't heard anything from them yet.'

Clive stopped scrolling through his emails. 'It went very well. Feldmann said he'd come back to me with feedback this afternoon.'

Palmer laughed, and leaned forward. 'Clive, they always say they'll come right back to you. If I had a quid for every time I'd heard that after a pitch....'

'No. Feldmann's an honourable bloke. He'll be in touch by end-of-play.'

Palmer stood up to leave. 'OK,' and he shrugged doubtfully. 'At any length, do let me know as soon as you hear. We'll need to talk. Plan.'

'We're already planning, Palmer. Think positive, hey?' He smiled, ignoring Palmer's smirk. 'Creative are well underway with the full blown presso for the next phase.' And he turned back to his email.

The MD had promised Clive this account would be his; but he worried that James McKinnie would not be strong enough to say no to Palmer. At 60, James McKinnie was looking forward to retiring to his house in the South of France. He'd lost interest in the company several years ago, but not quite enough to walk away just yet. When he'd turned 60, his lover, Paulo, begged him to retire, but it wasn't that easy: who would replace him? Clive imagined it would be Alex Palmer.

Palmer was fond of saying he 'lived and breathed media', but he was more emotional about his quarterly bonus. He was, like most of the middle management, adept at contorting income figures. He was also very good at concealing his outgoings – staff salaries, print costs, expenses. These were invisible to the dozy, middle-aged women in accounts, and even if they had wanted to question him, they would have been too afraid of his vicious temper. They preferred to leave it to their colleagues in the head office in Paris. At the end of each quarter, Palmer always issued a memo declaring record figures for his group.

Senior management sometimes queried the figures he submitted, but their greed, their desire to believe the numbers true, discouraged them from probing too deeply. And besides, trade press attention grew frenzied as AdVerbe announced another record year, and there were award dinners and client functions at newly launched bars and restaurants, and the thrill of riding high above London's media world distracted the managers long enough for Palmer to pocket yet another record bonus.

Before the sluggish, bureaucratic Paris-based head office could reach for its calculators, the next financial quarter was well under-way, and it was far too late to undo the miscalculations. Then Palmer would appear before the Board and help them to claw back the over spend – usually by suggesting that they 'let go' of another senior manager, or close down another group which was not performing as 'profitably' as his own. Other managers seethed at his arrogance, but none of them had the courage to confront him: despite his lack of height and his grey, alcoholic pallour, Palmer's lack of morals, scruples or empathy scared them. Clive called in the designers to go through the next phase of the pitch.

Just after 4pm, Gustav Feldmann emailed to say he and his colleagues were very pleased with AdVerbe's proposal and that they would like to proceed with the relationship; papers and contracts would follow via the usual routes. He expected to see Clive in Grenoble the day after tomorrow – a preliminary review of the creative before the official presentation in New York, the following week.

Clive emailed James McKinnie a brief note. 'I'll be with the team in the pub for the next hour or so, so let's meet tomorrow morning – when the paperwork gets here - and iron out the details – I want to move Palmer's team over to me as quickly as possible – Feldmann's will need a lot of energy.' He copied in Miranda and punched his middle finger on send.

*****

It was well after midnight when he stumbled in with the dog at his ankles, and fell on to the lounge where his wife was sleeping, waiting for him.

'I won!' he said, falling into her arms.

'I know,' Nic whispered. 'You called me – several times ...'

She tasted the whiskey on his breath when he kissed her. He slid his hands up under her T-shirt, and once again he was surprised by the intensity with which her body responded to his. Not long after, as she slept against his chest, the ansaphone wheezed into play.

'Nicola? I don't know if I have the right number? I'm looking for Nicola Steadman... um... sorry; Alwynn. Nicola Alwynn. Please call me...'

The American left his name – Michael Forester - and the number of his Park Lane hotel.

Clive lay awake in the darkness. There it was again: that shadow. This was Michael. Michael. Nic's lover from the States. Her ex-lover, he corrected himself. Clive had an image of him – tweedy; blonde; smug - bookish. He smiled to himself, and drew Nic closer.

Bella stirred on the rug and gave a small sigh of contentment. Clive reached over to erase the message.

*****

Nicole closed the book. It was 11 o'clock already and the postman shoved the letters through the door. She folded her glasses into their case and glanced down at the open manuscript:

I need to know
there's a hand breaking the ice
should I fall through.
To know, as I fall
from the bridge, you'll grip
my wrist firm; my body sways
in the safety of you. A branch
heavy with snow.

She pushed aside the duvet. Clive was long gone. He was so high on this win – she felt so happy for him, and she wondered if he knew that she supported him totally? She always felt that she couldn't say enough, do enough to reassure him - often she didn't know what to say. She wanted him to do well, to succeed, but she always felt a little guilty when he talked about his campaigns, because she'd lose interest just as quickly as he got fired up about it. She'd make it up to him tonight, they'd celebrate over dinner. She'd make pasta and salad – she had to go to the shops. She rolled out of bed, stepped into the shower and let her thoughts turn back to her research.

The village records ended in 1800, around the same time the village 'died', with the young all having moved to the larger, industrial centres – but she had found a Parnell, and a note of an Elizabeth, born to John and Sarah. Her Elizabeth? How many Elizabeths were born that year? Probably thousands, and Parnell was a common enough name in Derbyshire. How can we ever be sure, she thought, how will we know? That was the problem with Elizabeth: who was she? Who was the woman who wrote those amazing poems – 'poetic fragments', at least? And how did her journal turn up in San Francisco?

She sighed and bent down to pick up the letters from the front door mat. Maybe she should just give up on this whole thing, and concentrate on the teaching? Instantly, she felt her father's disapproval. He may have been dead for more than 20 years, but his hold over his only child had not diminished. She could almost smell the room he worked in, walls lined with books. If she closed her eyes she could run her hand along the back of his leather chair, or down the coat hanging on a hook on the back of the door. But even now, even in her imagination, she was afraid he might find her there.

And even when I yearn for light, my heart fears
the candle, the hearth. Even might the cold frostbite
at the softness, I turn away, choosing darkness lest he
see me,
or I his harsh rejection.

She stopped in the hallway; 'Even when I yearn for light...' she said out loud. Who was Elizabeth thinking of when she wrote these words? Her father? She shook her head to clear her mind, shuffled through the letters and poured herself a coffee, listening as the phone kicked into ansaphone mode. She always screened her calls, fearing a needy student in search of support.

There was a pause.

'Nicola?'... Nicola? It's me,' the American voice said.

The coffee machine made a loud, rude gurgle.

'Look – sorry. It's Michael…'

The silence was long, heavy.

Michael? The coffee cup dropped from her hand.

'Damn!' she grabbed the dishcloth and began mopping the floor.

'I'm sorry to bother you,' the message continued. 'But I'm in town for a few days – wondered if you'd like to catch up.' And he left the phone number of his hotel.

'Oh, great,' she thought as she rinsed out the cloth. 'Michael.'

How long had it been? Four, five years? She'd left in the morning, while Michael was at work, and flown home to London. She remembered the feeling of numbness as the cab driver loaded her suitcases into the boot, the note on the hall table, the flight from San Francisco, friends' spare rooms, applying for teaching jobs – and then Clive. She'd simply stopped thinking about Michael. Well, she didn't have time to think about him now. She had two classes to teach at the University, and she needed to have some time in the library this evening. Clive had said he'd be late. She hurried off to catch the bus.

All the way to the University, she struggled to keep thoughts of the past from her mind. The crisp chill to the air reminded her of her grandmother's house in the North - the silence of the place. The bare trees reminded her of winter in Virginia, her mother's room – empty, but still as it was when she'd died. And every blonde man made her think of Michael and driving up the coast in his convertible, the sea breeze rushing through her hair. She told herself to focus: she'd get through her two classes and retreat to the library, and Elizabeth's Derbyshire.

At 8pm, she realised with a start that she hadn't bought any food for tonight. She'd have to stop at the market near the bus-stop. Silent-footed librarians gathered up discarded books, arranging them alphabetically on their trolleys. Little breaths of snow flurried at the windows, melting in the watery orange of the security floodlights. Nicole clutched her books and hurried for the loans desk. Snow made the bus trip home slow, but there was a comfort in the warmth and silence of strangers, the windows misted over with breathing.

Bella's anxious face peered from the lounge window as she opened the gate. 'Here I am!' she called, and the dog spun away in a whirl of yelps and wagging tail. She unlocked the kitchen door and the dog exploded out into the night.

'What the ...?' She caught sight of the bins, both on their side, all the food scraps and paper recycling scattered across the lawn. 'Bloody foxes!' she shouted to the night. 'Damn it.' Well, she'd clear it up in the morning. 'Bella! Bella! Get away from there! Come inside...'

She put some water on to boil for the pasta, and made a simple salad, glad of the time to check her emails. She scanned the inbox – mainly students wanting to arrange appointments to discuss their essays, or begging for extensions to deadlines. These could wait until tomorrow. One from her agent – well, potential agent.

Marta Kaffner Associates was one of the most respected – if not most successful – literary agencies in the US. Nicole had studied with Marta's daughter, Tina, when they were post-grads in California. Nicole knew that Marta Kaffner would never have looked twice at her proposal without the Tina connection. God, she should email Tina.... it had been months.

Marta's Senior Editorial Assistant was clearly exasperated:

Dear Dr Alwynn,

As per our previous correspondence, we must now demand your proposal manuscript (promised to Ms. Kaffner some seven months ago).

As I am sure you will appreciate, Kaffner Associates (Agents Guild of America Literary Agency of the Year, 2010) guarantees not to approach publishers with any m/s that has not been thoroughly reviewed and evaluated by our panel of experts. Therefore, we cannot proceed without a detailed proposal.

Kaffner Associates receives more than two thousand submissions per month and we are forced to devote our resources to those authors who demonstrate total commitment and stamina.

Given the delay in your response, Ms. Kaffner has instructed me to ask you to submit within 14 days.

Should this prove impossible, we wish you every success in finding a more suitable Agency for your project.

Nicole sighed. Didn't these people realise how difficult this was? Elizabeth Parnell was not a movie star, she wasn't a pop singer. While there was, perhaps, a record of her birth, there was no record of her death. There was no marriage certificate, no known descendants. All that existed was one, precious, battered, leather-bound notebook. Not really a diary, although *some* days and events were recorded. Not really a collection of poetry, but, certainly, the fragments of poems jotted down in her confident, neat hand might constitute the beginnings of one. Elizabeth was proving elusive, and Nicole felt she really had nothing to show for her efforts of the last year. She'd avoided Kaffner Associates pushy emails, hoping for a breakthrough.

She scanned down the emails – one from the little museum she'd visited in Derbyshire in the summer. She braced herself for disappointment: *Further to your enquiry, we can confirm that an Elizabeth Jane Parnell (b.1738 – d. ?) travelled to the United States in 1758. We know this thanks to the Parish Council newsletter, which notes that the only daughter of Mr and Mrs John Parnell (he was a farmer – his property covering a considerable area) was sailing at month's end to join the family of her fiancé in America. California. We have no definite confirmation of exactly where, and no further references from the Parish newsletter (which, incidentally, ceased publication upon the death of the Vicar's wife, Mrs. Ann Rosswell, in 1770).*

She stared at the screen, unfolding the information slowly: her first real glimpse of Elizabeth.

She sensed, suddenly, her own grandmother's Derbyshire home where she'd spent her teens: grey stone sweating a damp, green cold and the rich, rain-sodden green hills falling toward it like a wave. The narrow stairs, the polished wood, the heavy drapes drawn across the draughty hallways. The feeling of fear and hope as you passed through them. Fear of what lay ahead, and the hope that it was not something terrible or fearful.

Have you seen
early morning glowing through the dark windows?
Remember me, then – and reach out –
remember I'm there behind you.

Clive would be home soon; she put the water to simmer and sat down to write a quick email to the Americans.

Dear Ms. Kaffner,

Please forgive the delay in my response – I won't bore you with all the reasons why. Suffice to say that a lecturer's life is a busy one, and the University has little concern for deadlines outside of its own.

Elizabeth Parnell has done her best to evade us but, as we know, that's always been her appeal. That said, the past months have unearthed some concrete facts that give real substance to the woman (please see attached correspondence).

I'm sure you'll see that this new information adds a real bonus in terms of selling to the US readership.

Ms. Kaffner, I am determined to send you a mostly complete proposal within the requested 14 days. As you know, I have decided to move away from the traditional, biographical approach and to focus, more, on the poetry itself – let the poetry (at least, fragments of it) tell Elizabeth's story. And, now, of course, I'd like to weave in the tale of her journey to the States.

One thing is certain, the journal covers an incredible time in both the US and the UK – a time of profound change for the world, for industry and especially for women.

Please accept this brief email as, firstly, an apology for my tardiness, and, secondly, a kind of insight into the complexities that this most amazing little book is throwing at me.

Please send your daughter my warmest regards.

Best wishes,

Nicole Alwynn (Ph.D.).

The snow had already turned to slushy half-formed flakes, and the passing car tyres made a soft, splashing sound. Bella barked loudly, making Nicole jump.

Clive stood in the hall and shook out his coat.

'Hey.' They embraced.

'You working hard?' he smiled.

'Hmmm?' She looked confused. 'Not really, I'm making supper!'

'With your reading glasses on?'

She smiled and blushed a little as she took her glasses off. 'OK – yeah. I got an email from that Library guy in Derbyshire… but, hey! I want to hear about your day. Come into the kitchen and talk to me while I cook.'

The water in the pasta pan had long steamed away.

'Oh, damn!' She grabbed the pot and turned off the burner.

'Here,' he laughed. 'Let me do it. You stick to the tomatoes…'

'Sorry. Anyway, tell me – what happened? Did James make the announcement? About you running the account?'

'Of course not – he was out all day. Bloody Palmer was prowling around like nobody's business.'

'What did you tell him?'

'Nothing – well, as little as I could. Just said I was off to Grenoble tomorrow to finalise some of the details…. The guy's an arsehole.'

'Yeah – certainly sounds like it. I can't believe how much crap he pulls. I mean, after that harrassment case – how can they trust him?'

'Anyway,' he shook the pasta into the boiling water. 'What's this news from Derbyshire?'

They talked over dinner. At midnight Clive yawned and said he'd have to get some sleep.

'What time is your flight?'

'After lunch – I'll leave from here.'

'So, you're staying the night?'

'Yeah. James recommended a hotel just outside of town. I'll be with Gustav for coffee next morning. He's got a house up in the mountains.'

'Let me clear the dishes and I'll follow you up – Bella's still out in the garden.'

Minutes later, the phone rang. She hurried to answer it before Clive had the chance to – his bloody office!

She held the phone long after Michael had rung off. 'Sure,' she'd whispered. 'That's fine.'

'I've got a few meetings,' he'd said. 'A drinks do at UCL - but they shouldn't run much after seven. No, don't worry – I'll take a cab.'

She stared out into the street.

She'd have to tell Clive before he left tomorrow morning. She could hardly wait until he got back from Grenoble and walked in to find her ex-lover at the dinner table. But she knew he'd take the news badly – he wouldn't say anything, but a cloud would pass over his face. He didn't like uncertainty; he didn't like changes to plans; he didn't like the unexpected. Darling Clive.

She'd met him three years ago. She'd been back in London almost a year, sleeping on her friend Cynthia's couch, and teaching part-time at the University of London.

Cynthia was a loud-mouthed American who'd brought the US idea of television book clubs to the UK. Over the past year, her recommendations, via a popular morning chat show, had firmly catapulted several mediocre novels into the Top 10 for weeks on end. Her lover at the time, Giles, was well on the way to entering that same stratosphere, with a murder mystery set between Bruges and London and featuring a romantic vision of the Eurostar, which had led to heavy endorsements, newspaper features and radio phone-ins, all offering return romantic journeys to Bruges and Lille. Cynthia had booked Giles onto chat shows for the next four weeks solid.

Of course, the highbrow critics were ready to tear the book to shreds – they loathed this American and her success. But it was water off a duck's back to Cynthia. At 45, she'd worked in publishing long enough to develop a very thick skin. Tall, very lean, her platinum blonde hair was cropped close, highlighting the sharp, hawkish contours of her face. But despite the harshness of her LA accent and the slash of pillar-box red lipstick, she was a warm and loving friend to a handful of people. Nicole had met her in San Francisco, when Cynthia was sharing an apartment with Michael's sister. Cynthia decided there and then that Nicole was to be the little sister she'd never had, and Nicole was happy to be adopted. By the time Nicole had fled San Francisco, Cyn had been living in London for nearly two years.

Cynthia had arranged a champagne launch for Giles' book – in an elegant bar just off Piccadilly Circus, and Nicole reluctantly agreed to drop by. It wasn't that she didn't want to celebrate her friend's success, but more that she'd shut down, and it was more than she could do to get out of bed every day and go through the motions.

'Come on, Nic? Please?' Cynthia had pleaded the night before. 'It will be fun! You haven't been out since you got here. Listen – it's no good moping over Michael. You said it yourself – it's over. Time to move on, girlfriend.'

Nicole wished she had been moping. Feeling anything would be better than this emotional nothingness. This void. She threw on jeans and a black cashmere jumper, wrapped her black coat tightly about her and headed for the party.

'Hey Nic! Glad you could make it!' Cynthia was all tight black trousers and a lightly woven black polo neck sweater, softened by a diamante crucifix tied tightly at the throat. She'd clearly had a glass or two of champagne. 'Giles? Giles?!' She shouted across the chatter and the piped music. 'Look – here's Nicole!'

Giles was deep in conversation with a tall, tired looking man. They suddenly laughed wildly at some private joke. Nicole liked the way the friend ran a broad hand through his wild shock of black hair, and the way he threw back his whiskey.

'Giles! Clive!' Cynthia shouted as she cut her way through the crowd, dragging Nicole behind her.

Clive turned to Cynthia, still laughing, but fell into stunned silence when he saw Nicole. Later, she laughed that it was as if he'd seen a ghost.

'Nicole, darling!' said Giles as he embraced her. 'Thanks for coming – Clive! Let me introduce you to Nicole – Nicole Steadman. Friend of Cyn's. Not a yank, though – well – maybe a little?'

'Oh. Shut up, Giles!' laughed Cynthia. 'Nicole – this is Clive Alwynn. He went to college with Giles.'

The room seemed to fade away a little as they reached out for one another's hands and Clive murmured something like 'How do you do / Nice to meet you.' She smiled uncertainly. 'Yes.'

Here I am, straining my hands through
a pond of green, soft darkness, hoping to reach you.

Bella barked somewhere in the darkness at the end of the garden. 'Bella! Bella! Come.' The dog ignored her and Nicole could hear a low growl through the darkness. 'Bella?' She grabbed the torch from the cupboard by the backdoor and stepped out into the darkness. 'Bella? Come!' Suddenly the dog was racing out of the darkness toward her, a huge ball of energy hurtling forward, but looking backwards nervously, barking loudly. Nicole laughed. 'Oh Bella! Who won? The fox or you?'

She locked the kitchen door, turned off the light and followed the growling dog upstairs. In the hush of the night, she felt like a child again – the lamp was on in the bedroom and a soft light glowed under the door. She felt anxious as she went in – like a bearer of bad-tidings. 'Say goodnight to your father, Nicole,' the nanny would say. And her father would look up from his book with a look of annoyance and – almost – fear, as his motherless child trembled in the doorway, a reminder of his loss.

She'd tell Clive about Michael tomorrow morning. For now, she was happy to watch him sleep - at peace and unafraid.

CHAPTER 2

It was already dark as Clive turned out of Lyon airport and joined the motorway to Grenoble. The Feldmanns owned houses all over the World – magnificent places, by all accounts – but Gustav Feldmann, the eccentric middle brother, preferred his comparatively small house in the grey mountains above Grenoble, at the foot of the Alps.

His wife had died six years ago, and now, at 78, Gustav felt jaded by the bank and its machinations. That was not to say he took no interest in the business. He had to. His eldest brother, Alonso, was fading away in Montreux. At 85, he floated in and out of lucidity under the watchful eyes of a team of 24-hour carers, propped up in a pneumatic bed that overlooked the cold blue surface of Lake Geneva.

The youngest Feldmann, Walter, seemed much younger than his 66 years. Married to a Filipino – Jenelyn – he moved a small entourage from home to home in his private jet. More interested in movies than banking, his film company, Asian Flowers, produced hard-core productions using questionably young girls from Manila and Bangkok.

Walter's wife, at 20 too old to interest her husband any longer, was able to turn a blind eye to his activities in return for a sizeable monthly payment from the Bank. (Although once, finding her husband in a Jacuzzi with a thirteen-year-old, she had almost drowned the child, and then cracked a half-empty champagne bottle across Walter's head. He was rushed to hospital, unconscious, and the papers reported the next day that Walter Feldmann was making a full recovery after a nasty fall at his Swiss home. His devoted wife was at his side.)

Walter never attended the monthly Board meetings in Paris, and he rarely responded to correspondence from the Executive, but as an equal partner in the bank, no decisions could be made without his sign-off.

Clive checked into the hotel his Director had recommended, just on the outskirts of Grenoble. James had described it as 'old-worldly', 'elegant', 'classy', but the empty swimming pool, its sides mosaiced in the skeleton stains of orange and brown leaves, the wrought iron garden chairs rusting at the joints, the garden frosted with a layer of snow, and the windows dully lit with power-saving bulbs, made him anxious.

He shuddered. Just one night – then tomorrow he'd drive up into the mountains and talk Gustav Feldmann through his ideas for the new campaign. In his room, he opened up the folio and spread the creative boards across the modest double bed. The dull light did nothing for the colours, but he knew the outline of every frame almost by heart.

So why didn't he feel that rush, that kick in the guts that told him this was it, this was *the* idea?

'Oh, fuck it,' he sighed. He was tired. It was late. He'd already won the bloody account. This was simply a formality. He needed to go and find the restaurant – *'Michelin Star!'* James had trilled. And he needed to call Nic.

Looking around the shabby room, with its mélange of tastes and styles, all grouped under the umbrella of 'antique', he smiled to think that this 'oldness' would interest her. She'd insist on finding romance in it, look for a story in it. But for him, it was nothing but a decrepit and badly put together room, and it made him feel lonely.

His childhood memories were of stuffy, cold, long hallways, early morning running barefoot for the shower. He remembered dusty photographs, their frames peeling, old lampshades sitting slightly askew on plastic, brass-look bases. He'd been fostered to several homes when he was younger, but it always turned out badly, and he was always returned to the orphanage with a sense of terrible failure. It seemed he had 'behavioural problems' - he was always defiant or 'oppositional'. As a small boy, he'd marvelled at his own inability to communicate, the way that everything he said seemed to have the opposite effect on the adults around him. In rare moments of happiness, he'd wonder why no one around him shared the joke, or why they'd suddenly banish him from the room.

He snapped open his mobile and pressed Nicole's speed dial. Straight to ansaphone. He'd forgotten – it was nearly midnight in London; she was undoubtedly asleep - bedside lamp on, glasses halfway down her nose, Sebastian the cat curled tightly at the foot of the bed. He left a message.

'Nic, honey? It's me. Realise you're asleep. Ummm….. Sorry – long day. I'll call you when I finish with Feldmann tomorrow. Hey – you'd love this hotel. I love you.'

CHAPTER 3

Virginia Alwynn liked to laugh at New York; laugh at the utter rigidness of this 'newest' democracy. The land of the free was just as narrow and as stifling as her Hampshire, UK, childhood had been.

Some days she longed for a damp, grey sky and the surly indifference of fellow-commuters on the Northern Line. Ridiculous, she knew; she remembered long months of a deep, bone-heavy depression, and an ever-present sense of dread that characterised the days – even after the boys – when things were at their happiest.

'Enough!' she admonished herself. She took the speed of the treadmill down to 5k, breathing heavily after the sprint. There was no denying that leaving London had been the hardest thing she'd ever had to do. 'But it's too late to turn back now,' she said, as she went to shower. Her mother and father called every weekend to try and persuade her to come home.

'We miss the boys, darling – and you, of course. You could all move back in here. It's just daddy and I rattling around now.'

She loved her parents. She worried about them, and what would happen when one of them died or they became too frail to care for themselves – but that was some way down the road, she hoped. And the thought of moving back to her childhood home seemed something like a defeat.

It had taken well over a year for her and the boys to make a new life here. She had the job, a good apartment on the East Side, corporate membership to one of the best gyms in New York, and an analyst who, unlike his English counterparts, didn't argue with the conclusions she'd reached between midnight and 4am.

This life was so different to the one she had in London, but it was a life – the only one she had. Over the months, she thought of Clive less often. She scheduled essential dates into her calendar, and Melanie, her P.A., sent cards and photos from the boys as per the divorce settlement.

Be damned if she'd stay trapped in the past. She was 43 years old. Life was too short.

She spent the day working on layouts for a new women's magazine for the 'single, separated or divorced'. She wondered if Jonathan, the Publisher, hadn't asked her to work on it because of her own situation, but brushed aside the idea that she was perceived as anything other than a bloody good designer.

She shut down her computer just after 6 and flagged a cab home. The boys were bathed and fed, laughing hysterically. She knew Rachel would have insisted they finish their homework, even if that meant allowing them to work in front of the television. She disapproved, but had never had the heart – or the courage – to confront her. So long as it was done.

Rachel was shaking the dishwater from the rubber gloves. She was an aspiring writer with a Diploma in childcare. Thirty-seven, overweight, short, with wild threads of gun-metal grey shooting from a heavy mane of rich brown hair which she struggled to keep in a loose knot at the nape of her neck. She lived two blocks away from Virginia and the boys and had become, to Virginia's occasional irritation, the lynchpin of their new life.

'Hey, Mrs Alwynn. The school's sent some forms home to be signed – there, on the sideboard. Trip to the museum. Jack's been invited to another birthday party – Friday – 3-5 – I can pick him up, of course. I'll get a gift tomorrow. I've folded the wash. We had chicken – there's some cold cuts in the fridge. Try and eat something! See you tomorrow morning.'

Ben and Jack were huddled on the sofa. Their blonde hair – so wild and free-willed, no matter how hard you combed it – was still damp at the forehead after their bath. They smelled like mild, white bubbles and towels straight off the heated rail.

'Hey you two! No kisses for your poor mother?'

Jack dragged himself away from the screen and kissed her on the cheek. Ben sort of waved and blew her a kiss, interrupted by a loud guffaw.

'Look, Jack! They ran him over!'

Jack ran back to the sofa.

'Hmmmm. Bed in 20 you guys,' she said as she went to the kitchen, ignoring their complaints and shuffling through the day's post. Nothing of interest. She glanced at the ansaphone as she poured a glass of wine. Two messages.

The first was from Matthew, asking her to dinner. Again. She had to hand it to him – he was resilient. Ever since her colleague Angie had set them up over dinner, she'd been avoiding his calls and emails. There was nothing wrong with him – in fact, she thought, he was remarkably healthy and intelligent for a single man in New York, and a good seven years younger than her. An accountant. Divorced. Two kids. Why didn't she just relax and say yes to dinner? The boys guffawed from the lounge.

'OK, boys! Bed! I'll come and tuck you in in 5....'

The next message was from Clive. She stared at the machine.

'*Hi, Ginnie. It's Clive. Listen – I wanted to talk to you. I might be in New York next week...... Don't know if you're free – ummmm. Maybe we could meet up. Ummmm. I'd love to see the boys. .... I know it's been a while, but...*'

And the message cut out.

Way below, down in the street, a siren wailed. She pressed delete and went to settle the boys. Later, sitting alone in the lounge, she had another glass of wine and wondered why Clive's call had made her so angry. They'd agreed some time before that communication had to be limited to email, and to be kept business-like and to the point. They were incapable of having a civilised conversation – even about the boys. And after he'd remarried, he'd rarely bothered to respond to her brief notes about the boys' school results or visits to doctors/dentists. It had been understood that Clive would visit New York to see them – maybe once or twice a year. But after a couple of abortive attempts – she had a new launch, he had a big pitch – he seemed to give up. She was afraid of the distress his visit would create. Jack and Ben would want him to stay, but of course he wouldn't. He had a wife and home to go to.

She sighed, turned off the lamp, and half-dozed until the early, grey dawn. She'd email Clive today – she could hardly stop him from seeing the boys if he was here in New York, but she could do some damage limitation. He could come here to the apartment, have dinner and then go away. Simple.

She made a mental note to cook the lamb ragout the night before. It would flavour and settle well over the day. Clive adored her cooking.

She made a pot of tea and looked out across the mosaic of windows. All over the city the world was waking up, ready for the fight. She smiled to herself. What would her Cognitive Therapy guy say about that? 'OK,' she said out loud. 'All over the city, people are waking to embrace the day!' And she decided she'd take Matthew up on his offer of dinner.

She went to the kitchen and rattled the cat's biscuit tin - 'Mr Porky!' The doorbell rang – 6am on the dot. Rachel was better than anything Greenwich could offer.

'Hey Mrs Alwynn.'

After Virginia had washed and dressed, Rachel had already set the boys' breakfast on the small table in the kitchen and made their beds. As Virginia called 'Goodbye!' and closing the door behind her, Rachel was dressing the boys and packing their bags for the school day ahead.

'Bye Mrs Alwynn!'

'Oh, Rachel? Is there a chance you can mind the kids one night this week? I may have a dinner...'

CHAPTER 4

Clive reached from the car window and pressed the buzzer at the security gate – nothing fortress-like, just a simple wrought iron gate that jerked with a stutter, hesitated, then slowly glided open, making a wave through the fallen snow and leaves.

As the car rounded the curving drive, Gustav strode from the house, two dizzy red setters weaving about his legs. He was a tall man, moving a little more slowly than he might have twenty years ago, but still strong and vital.

'Ahh, so you found us!' called Gustav.

'It was the name on the gate that gave it away,' laughed Clive, as they shook hands and the dogs jumped up between them. 'Hello, dog!'

'Get down, Angel! Blue! Sorry, they don't see many visitors nowadays. We bought them as guard dogs – bloody waste of money! No, leave your bags, George will bring them in – George!'

A small man in his fifties appeared from the house.

'George – bring in Mr Alwynn's bags and please tell your wife we will eat in one hour. She can bring whiskey to the sitting room now.'

They squeezed through the narrow hallway, the dogs sliding recklessly across the rugs, surfing the polished wood floor.

'Get down!' shouted Gustav. 'Let me take your coat, Clive. Get down! George! Come and take the bloody dogs! Quick Clive – in here ...'

Clive was pushed gently into a large, brightly lamp-lit sitting room. At one end a huge curtainless window framed a breathtaking view of mountains.

A fire burned quietly, opposite a long sofa. In the corner, there was a huge leather chair set in front of a broad, low coffee table covered with heavy-looking reference guides and a laptop. Gustav retrieved his glasses from the coffee table, and tucked them into his jacket pocket.

'Sit down, sit down,' he said, gesturing toward the sofa.

'God – it's beautiful,' sighed Clive, tearing himself away from the spectacular view.

'Yes. One never gets used to it – it's different every time. Sometimes it's quite new. Did you have a pleasant trip?'

'Oh, yes – the drive from Lyon ...'

George's wife entered with a tray, and the dogs slipped in behind her, slinking to the rug in front of the fire.

Gustav cleared newspapers from a small table to the right of the sofa.

'Just here, please Madame Géroux.'

Mme. Géroux nodded to Clive, and then spoke discreetly to Gustav.

'Mais oui!' he cried. 'The 1973 Merlot – I trust the lamb is worthy of it?'

Mme. Géroux raised her chin in a defiant, yet indulgent, gesture.

'It has never been unworthy in 25 years, Monsieur,' she huffed as she left the room.

'Wonderful woman. She and her husband have been with us since I married – 25 years ago.'

He noticed Clive's frown. 'Yes – I married late. Lilliana – Lilli – was my second wife, God rest her. We came to look at this house on a whim – we were staying with friends in Grenoble and they mentioned a holiday place for sale. George and his wife were caretaking the place until a sale was secured. Lilli and Mme. Géroux took to each other immediately – Lilli was 43 and Madame . . . 30 maybe? (I've always been too afraid to confirm!) We bought the house immediately and the Géroux have called it home ever since.'

'That's very generous of you,' smiled Clive.

'Not at all. Before Lilli fell ill, we were often away. Business, the bank. Someone needed to be here – security, the dogs. Lilli missed them so much when we were away … '

He stared at the snowy mountain peaks as they drifted in and out of the settling cloud.

'Anyway,' he coughed. 'Damn waste of money. Don't know how she ever thought they'd make good guard dogs. Stupid creatures,' he smiled, stroking one of the silky heads. 'Lunch will be served shortly – after that, we'll go to the study and go through these new ideas of yours. We have a conference call with the Board tomorrow – I'd like to have their buy-in before you leave. What time is your flight?'

CHAPTER 5

The hostess was passing hot towels and beaming in that toothy way Business Class hostesses do. He pressed the towel to his face and took a moment to enjoy the stillness.

The meeting with Gustav had been intense, if not entirely successful. Gustav had listened politely as Clive presented the campaign, nodding occasionally, jotting notes, and making small encouraging sounds. But Clive sensed his reticence well before he came to the last creative board.

'I appreciate what your team has done, Clive, and I understand what you tried to do. You don't focus on the Bank's past, and you've not forced us into the 'future'. But I have a feeling that ….. I think we should show some sort of link between the past and the future? A connection. Does that make any sense? At the moment, I see three distinct Feldmann's: the past, now, tomorrow. I don't see what's holding them together…'

Despite an instinctive desire to argue the point, Clive found himself nodding slowly. Gustav was right. Clive had paid nothing but lip service to the old Feldmann's, dismissed it in a sepia-toned freeze frame. And the truth was that he didn't really get what the connection was. He found it frustrating to even begin to articulate – even to himself.

'No point in presenting it to the Board just yet,' smiled Gustav gently. 'I suggest you go back to London, fine-tune it – and please don't think it's all entirely wrong. The work is excellently presented. We'll take it to the Board next week. We're meeting in New York for the Exec, anyway.'

Clive made the 17.30 and stared vacantly at the hostess going through the safety procedures.

'Don't forget,' she smiled. 'The nearest exit might be behind you.'

He was exhausted, and her words were dancing about in his head in crazy ways.

'Should you hear the words "Brace. Brace." The position to adopt should oxygen masks fall from the overhead locker.'

Sipping his champagne, he looked out at the darkening rose and grey skyline. He wondered if Virginia had picked up his message yet? Would she be pleased? Would she call him? What if she didn't? Would this be the first standoff? Would he have to call his lawyer? Sure, she'd be surprised, but he'd tried to see the boys more often – but with work and the distance. It wasn't every day he had a meeting in New York.

And tomorrow night he had dinner with Nic's ex-lover. 'You'll never guess who called,' she'd said over coffee yesterday morning. Like most things about Nic's past, he found the prospect of Michael unsettling. He wasn't afraid, and besides, he made a rule of never being jealous. He simply never considered her past, as if, by ignoring it he cancelled out its existence. So to have a piece of it turning up at his dinner table was disturbing. He signalled to the hostess.

'Whiskey, please. No ice.'

He sat back with his eyes closed and recalled the first night he'd met Nic – at Giles's book launch. He'd already knocked back too much whiskey – there was rarely a moment with

Giles in the last twenty years when he hadn't been drunk. But the moment he turned and saw Nic standing there, he was stone cold sober.

She looked startled. It was January outside and the cold had left a dark pink flush up both of her cheeks. There was nothing extraordinary about her face – she wasn't unattractive – but there was nothing exceptional. It was something else, something in the depth of her brown eyes. She was clearly uncomfortable in the crowd, voices rising above the generic jazz.

Months later, when they married at the Hackney Town Hall, she'd turned to face him with that same look in her eyes and he knew this was the right thing to do.

Even now, a little drunk and a little tired as the plane touched down at Stansted, he could close his eyes, recall that look, and find a stillness and a safety he'd never known before.

He'd play the perfect host tonight – the perfect husband – and he would send this Michael on his way and lock the door behind him.

CHAPTER 6

Michael Forester woke early. 'As a matter of habit...', he sighed, dismissing the cliché. He stared up at the unfamiliar hotel ceiling. *Was* this a habit? Or was it the price he paid for being successful? Was he condemned to living in other people's time zones?

He'd grown used to the ritual: eyes open, grey light, unfamiliar ceiling. Now, as a matter of course, every night before he turned off the lamp, he left his return ticket on the bedside table, folded open on the details page.

He reached over and answered the buzzing phone: the automated voice said it was now 5am, and this was his wake-up call. An American accent, like every other hotel in the world. He reached across for the ticket – San Francisco - London – San Francisco. He was in London. Of course.

Somewhere, maybe 30 minutes away by black London taxi, he imagined Nicola was deep in sleep; a book fallen into her lap, glasses slipping down her nose. The thought unnerved him. He sat up too quickly, held his head in his hands, regretting last night's lonely drinking session.

Room service arrived. He gulped down the coffee, and booted up his laptop. At 9.30 he'd be delivering his first lecture – the last one finished just after 7. He'd just published his fourth book. Pretty much a rehash of his previous three books, it questioned the relationship of everyday language to poetry. Was poetry simply a different way of using everyday language? Or was it an entirely new language? If so, what separated poets from the rest of us? He mixed linguistic theory with biography and poems and concluded, in each book, that poetry was an unsolvable mystery. Of course, he threw in enough contentious declarations to ensure that the grandees of the academic world were up in arms and, so, his book – and he – became an essential presence at conferences, salons and dinner parties.

He went over his notes and breathed out angrily. This is mad, he thought. He drew back the nylon curtains and stared across a dismal London landscape. She *can't* be happy here. He thought about the view across the Bay from their lounge, the long, hot summer evenings when the muslin curtains sighed lazily into the room on the soft breeze.

Nicola. He felt the familiar sense of having lost something... the sudden, knee-jerk panic that parents must feel in supermarkets when they look down to see their child gone. And, as always, it disoriented him. No, he thought, as he paced the room. This was his chance. For closure – no matter which way it went. All he knew for certain was that he had to see her. He needed her to... what?

He switched on CNN, and switched it off. He flicked through the newspaper they'd left outside his door. Despite the double-glazing and despite being on the fourth floor, London's traffic hummed a grey wall of sound. He fell back on to the bed, playing her words over and over again, examining each hesitation, each pause, each rush to fill the silent gaps with something 'safe'.

'Hello!' she'd said after the initial shock. 'What? In London? God – wonderful.'

So here they were – Nicola inviting him to dinner. He knew she'd wanted to laugh at the awkwardness as much as he did.

As he lay in bed afterwards, he'd imagined her mouth close to the phone. Those lips and the places they'd explored, and here they were – Nicola inviting him to dinner, formally, politely, confirming the unbreachable distance that time had built between them.

'Clive's in France, but he'll be back the day after tomorrow. So... we'll see you then.'

He'd only seen one picture of Clive. Nicola had sent a wedding photo with a brief note to say she hoped all was well with him, etc.

He guessed Clive was around 6'3", nearly a half-foot taller than Michael. Clive had a wild sweep of thick black hair; Michael's was a fine, wheat-field blonde and cut very short. Michael's eyes behind his glasses were a pale sky blue. Clive's dark eyes laughed back at the camera with an intensity and, thought Michael, a coarseness, that made Michael flinch.

Breathing in the steam of the bathwater rushing through the brass taps, he watched his face disappear in the foggy mirror. He ran a hand across the grey hair on his chest. He imagined Clive was fit and strong, his muscles always tense and taut, ready to pounce – to fight.

He sighed deeply; he had never wanted to fight – at least not that he remembered. And now he was too old and too tired to try. What had happened to him? What had happened to all the ambition, all the drive, that had seen him heading up the Literature department at Stanford well before his 40th birthday?

What had happened to his need for women, young eager students – who looked at him as though he was God? Oh sure, they still threw themselves at him, but it all seemed so empty now.

He gathered his cashmere coat about him and braced himself for the day ahead. If he could get through this, then he could hurry back to the hotel, order a large bottle of whiskey, and lay back in his bath, thinking of Nicola and preparing himself for their dinner. Her husband would be no more than a mild distraction once Michael started telling her about his latest work.

CHAPTER 7

Alex Palmer woke around 4am – he blinked his eyes, confused and wondering where he was. Becca stirred beside him.

'Shit!' he thought. 'Shit!'

He slipped out of bed and crept away. He found the bathroom and washed his face, slicking back his hair.

'Shit!' He looked terrible, all puffy eyes and grey-toned skin, and he thought he might throw up.

He slipped out of the front door and hurried into the street. Where the fuck was he? Think! Rebecca, lived in... North London! Yes, he was in Finsbury Park.

He scanned the text messages on both phones. He'd set up a second number a month ago. Esther seemed to be *too* aware of his movements, where he was, who he was seeing – not that she knew about the girls. Jesus. If she – or her father – ever found out about his little sorties, he'd be stuffed. He'd lose the house, the car, everything her money had bought him. Palmer was prone to paranoia, but he was certain that someone was watching him – particularly on those long nights in the pub. Those long, lost nights that always started with a lunchtime drink and inevitably finished the next morning in a strange bed.

Esther would be livid – she'd sulk for a day, but eventually she'd believe his story of a late night at work, a few drinks and crashing out on a mate's lounge room floor.

'Never again,' he said as he flagged a lone cab cruising down the Holloway Road. This had to stop, he told himself. Hadn't he had enough trouble with that little bitch accusing him of harassment? And then Debs, the silly tart who'd mistaken a couple of drunken shags for some kind of grand passion.

He kept a change of clothes and a hip flask in his locker at a gym on the Tottenham Court Road, close to the office. A shower, a coffee, a shot of Resolve and a hair of the dog, and he'd be as good as new.

What was happening today? Think... He scrolled through the emails on his Blackberry.

One of his phones rang, and he opened it absentmindedly. 'Esther? Darling, I'm *so* sorry, I...'

Becca sighed. 'It's me, Alex. Where'd you get to?'

'Oh, Becca – ha! – I'm ahh, I'm at the office. Lots to do, you know!'

'Look Alex, you were welcome to stay for coffee. I just wanted to let you know I won't mention last night – it'll be between us. I mean it's not as if anything *happened*.'

Palmer stared at the passing traffic. He imagined she smirked as she said nothing happened. Of course nothing *happened* – apart from the fact he was a happily married man, and he'd sack the little bitch if she tried to upset that – they were both completely inebriated. Of course nothing happened.

'Thanks, Becca. God! I have a stinking hangover. What time you in? Nine I hope – you know how essential punctuality is! I want even higher margins this week. You guys are on a roll.'

He snapped his phone shut.

He opened the message from James. Ahhh, yes. Now he remembered. James had forwarded him a message from Alwynn – looked like Alwynn had fucked up the Feldmann's account.

To:	James.Mckinnie@AdVerbe.com
From:	*Clive.Alwynn@AdVerbe.com*

Hi James,

At the airport on my way back.

I took Feldmann through the boards – he was impressed.

He has one worry – and I think I agree with him. I'll be in tomorrow, and I'll brief the team then. In a nutshell: we need to get more of a connection between the three pieces – past, present, future. All one. All together.

One of the obstacles may *be that we don't have enough from Feldmann's as to exactly what their 'now' is? I put this to Gustav and he and I are meeting in NY early next week to discuss. I'll be back at home tonight if you need to discuss.*

Palmer smirked. He'd never liked Clive Alwynn. Of all the Executives, only Alwynn had ever challenged the reports

Palmer had handed to the Board every three months. He remembered him laughing out loud as Palmer presented his record-breaking figures for Q2.

He was waiting in Clive's office when he arrived at 8.15.

'Oh. Hello Palmer, how are you? And what are you doing in my office?'

'Oh, I'm fine, thanks – thought we'd get an early start on sorting out this Feldmann's review.'

Clive smiled, and hung up his coat. 'No need for you to worry, really. Just a few tweaks we need to go through...'

'Sounds like more than just a few 'tweaks', Clive.'

He saw Clive's surprise... 'Yes, James forwarded me your message. Asked me to take it from here ...'

Clive flushed angrily. 'Well, let's go and talk to James, shall we?'

'I have a meeting with him later, so I can...'

'No!' Clive slammed his hand down on the desk. 'I want us to both go and see James and see how this is going to work.'

'That's exactly it, Clive,' Palmer moved toward the door, a little afraid. 'I'm here to make it work.'

'No, Palmer. This is my account. And the sooner you're away from it, the better.'

Palmer laughed. 'Oh, Clive. Don't take it so personally. It's not about *you*. It's about Feldmann's. Let's go talk to James, hmmm?' And he smiled.

James McKinnie looked up from the morning paper, as Palmer and Clive walked in to his office. 'Oh, God,' he thought. 'Just what I need at 8.30 in the bloody morning, an executive bloody showdown.'

There were six senior executives, but James only rated two of them: Palmer and Janie McDonough. Palmer was brash, unpredictable, and there had been that unfortunate episode with one of the junior sales girls. She'd threatened to sue and walked away with a considerable pay-off. But James believed Palmer might turn himself around now that he'd married. He liked Janie, but as she'd been pregnant two out of the last four years, he really couldn't see her as MD material.

Some of the Board rated Clive Alwynn, but Alwynn had always baffled James. It wasn't his unconventional approach, it was more his… remoteness? Oh, he was perfectly affable – but there was a distance that made James uneasy. James smiled as he remembered Paolo's summation of last year's Christmas party photos. '*That Clive Al-wynn,*' he'd pouted. '*He's just too handsome not to be up to something*!'

'Gentlemen, come in,' he said without smiling. 'Clive – how was Grenoble?'

Palmer sank into the large, red leather sofa. 'Well, I think we know how it went already, James…'

Clive smiled, and sat opposite James. 'Yes, James. Palmer tells me you'd like him to take the account from here on?'

James sat back and sighed. 'Now Clive, don't get all steamed up. I simply asked Palmer to keep an eye on things – just to start. He has a little more experience than you and I'd like him to...'

'James,' Clive interrupted quietly. 'I have not worked my arse off for AdVerbe for the last three years to be told that I am not experienced enough to run this account.'

'No one is saying that Clive! It's just that this is a very 'delicate' account. Old Europe, old money... Feldmann's will need a ... shall we say ... a little more *finesse* than our previous City clients.'

'Oh cut the Public School crap, James. I've spent the last two months courting Gustav Feldmann and the only finesse he needs is transparency and honesty. Not something I'd associate with a Public School education,' and he looked to Palmer.

James sighed. 'Clive... look....'

'No, James. I've been clear from the start. This is my account I won it.'

'Well,' smiled Palmer. 'Not quite, yet. Plenty of time to fuck it up.'

'I have no intention of fucking it up, Palmer.'

'Well, it might be worth remembering,' and Palmer stood up, 'to get sign off on budgets next time.'

Clive looked confused, as Palmer perched on James' desk. 'I spoke to Finance yesterday – it seems you went in way under … not good. Not good at all.'

'Yes,' James agreed. 'We need to milk this one, Clive. You see? That's exactly why you need Palmer onside.' He saw Clive's fists clench. 'Don't worry – it's your account. You can have the team – I'll make an announcement immediately. Congratulations. I think you and Palmer can really make this work.'

'That's all I want,' smiled Palmer.

Clive stood up to leave. 'Thank you James. I'll keep you updated.' And he strode from the room.

Palmer sighed. 'I'll keep an eye on it James… he really has to learn to calm down, you know.'

James grunted and turned back to his paper.

Palmer spent the rest of the morning on the Feldmann's site. Crap, he decided. Then at lunchtime he went across the road to the pub.

The girls from ad sales were gathered at the bar laughing loudly.

'Alex?' Kirsty shouted. 'What are you having?'

Kirsty, the new sales girl, had just landed a four-issue deal with Viola hair care products – this one campaign would guarantee another four issues of the glossy franchise magazine. Palmer was already adding income to this quarter's spreadsheet.

He watched her order another round, flirting with the Brazilian barman. She was blonde and very good-looking in a Counties way. She wore tight trousers and a low cut top beneath a tightly tailored jacket. Business, yet sexy. She could go a long way, he smiled, and, unconsciously smoothed back his thinning hair.

Esther wouldn't expect him back until 7. He'd leave the car at the office overnight, and take a cab home. He hated these office gigs – really. He didn't notice Debs, chatting amiably with some of the team at the other end of the bar.

Deborah Curtis hated Palmer. She watched him fawn over the new girl, watched the way the other girls vied for his attention. 'Look at him,' she told herself. She wanted to understand why she'd even bothered with him.

He was around 5' 7", about a stone overweight, puffy, and stank of stale cigarette smoke. He spoke quickly, agitatedly, in a public school accent that belied his lower middle-class education at a local comprehensive.

Their affair had lasted for an intense and exhausting four months. What she'd thought would be a career-boosting one-night stand turned into something much darker. Palmer was high-maintenance – long, late nights of drinking and self-pity. He'd told her he loved her and that he was unhappy in his marriage. He'd told her about his awful childhood – his alcoholic mother and his ineffectual father. He'd told her about his wealthy uncle and the inheritance he was still fighting for. He stayed at her flat several nights a week and she took to washing his shirts in her bathroom basin, while he lay nearly comatose on the bed.

She didn't love Palmer; but the morning she heard one of the girls gossiping in the toilet, laughing at the fact that Palmer 'could not get it up', she realised she'd allowed herself to be used. It seemed they all knew his secret.

The sales girls laughed with delight as Palmer half fell from his bar stool, falling into Kirsty's arms. His wife texted again. It was 7pm. The sales girls said their goodnights and wandered out, but Kirsty sat patiently at the bar. He switched off his phone. Esther would have to wait.

CHAPTER 8

'The lengths people go to in order to hide,' thought Jay Swift, as he trawled through the rubbish bin. 'Forget firewalls. Forget passwords. Forget unlisted numbers. People had no idea how much of their lives was splayed open in the wheelie bin at the end of their garden.' He laughed silently. This visit alone would allow him to put together quite a comprehensive picture of the woman: she was not interested in getting pregnant (the used condoms, the absence of pregnancy testing kits); he guessed she used tampons as there were no pads evident; she was careful about her appearance – so many creams and such, and vitamins. She used low-fat milk and drank herbal teas. She also went through a truck-load of painkillers and antacids. Nervous type.

He moved silently to the recycling bins; loads of bottles – lots of drinking went on here; then the paper bin. What was this? He couldn't see in the half light, and he didn't want to risk turning on his torch. He shoved the sheets of paper into his jacket, hurried up the path and out onto the street. He knew that this level of detail was so much more than his Client had requested, but Jay Swift was not a man who did things by halves. He'd been asked to track the man, but he knew from experience that he'd learn more about the man by learning about his woman. Or his women, as the case may be. Back in the car, he looked through the crumpled pages. 'Well, well, well,' he smiled. 'What do we have here?'

CHAPTER 9

Bella bounced and barked at the front window. Nicole stopped re-arranging the lilies on the dining room table. The doorbell sounded and she checked the hall clock – 7pm. Michael was, as always, punctual.

Damn. Clive was late. She glanced around the room: lights quite low, chillout on the CD, all casual and easy.

'Bella! Bella! Come!' and she locked her in the kitchen.

She looked quickly at her reflection in the hall mirror, smoothed down her t-shirt and opened the front door.

Michael hadn't changed a bit. She was always amazed that he could travel halfway around the world and back and still look like he'd had a great night's sleep.

Blonde, handsome, with the threat of coldness in his eyes, she could see why she'd been attracted to him. Before she'd had a chance to say anything, Clive's taxi appeared in the drive.

'Oh, goodness!' she smiled apologetically at Michael. 'My husband's just arrived! Please do go through – I won't be a second.' And she hurried down the drive Michael turned quickly enough to see Clive hurriedly turn away, pretending that he hadn't been sizing him up. He went through into the lounge, where a bottle of wine and three glasses was waiting on the coffee table. He undid his coat, listening to Nicola's laughter as she walked Clive through to the lounge.

'Come in and meet our guest, darling. Michael, this is my husband – Clive.' Clive imagined he saw Michael wince, but shrugged it off, striding forward, reaching out his hand.

'Clive,' Michael nodded. 'Nice to meet you at last.'

'Yes.' Clive noticed the wine bottle and glasses. 'Michael, I'm assuming you're a wine man – we don't have California, but France do a nice line in reds. Nic, honey, I'll have a whiskey, I think.'

'Of course,' she smiled. 'Michael, let me take your coat, and, sit down. You're not allergic to dogs are you? I hope not – Bella will never forgive us if she doesn't get to meet a new person!'

Bella barked loudly from the kitchen, and they all laughed. 'Let me get your whiskey, and let her out!'

Clive yawned, and fell back into a lounge chair.

'Long day, Clive?' Michael asked.

'God, yes – I don't know why they insist on so much security checking on a flight back from Lyon – it was clearly returning business people – and then the bloody driver didn't turn up. The company's changed to a cheaper firm. I'm sorry – I'm not always ranting like this!'

He looked to Nic for confirmation as she passed him his drink, and perched on the arm of the sofa. She smiled comically, rolling her eyes.

'Ok! Ok! I am, but – enough already! Michael – Nic tells me you're based at Stanford. What brings you to London?'

Michael was sitting in the long sofa by the side window; a soft orange glow from the streetlight gave the effect of a halo. He looked directly at Clive, half smiling, gently rolling the wine in his glass.

'Yeah. I've been at Stanford forever – since Nicola left ...' He glanced at Nicole. 'I've just published a book, and a couple of Universities over here asked me to come talk about it.'

Nicole laughed. 'He's being terribly modest, Clive! This is Michael's fourth book, and if the previous three are anything to go on, I reckon it's bound to be another best-seller.'

'Well,' interrupted Michael. 'At least in the academic world!' He grimaced, feigning embarrassment.

'Nonsense!' she laughed, topping up his wine, and then her own. Clive noticed she seemed to be a little too drunk already, and wondered why she'd needed an earlier shot of Dutch courage. 'Clive? Have I told you about the course Michael taught on Auden?'

'No.' Clive rose abruptly. 'What's for dinner, Nic? Can I do anything? Forgive me, Michael, but I am famished.'

Nicole frowned, 'No, everything's underway.' She excused herself, and went to the kitchen.

'Auden?' asked Clive. 'I thought you were a linguistics prof?' he asked, play-wrestling Bella to the floor.

'Sure,' smiled Michael. 'We don't make that distinction between poetry and linguistics in the States.'

'Oh no! No you don't! I know better than to get into that sort of debate with you academics! But,' he finished off his whiskey, 'I guess it all boils down to words, at the end of the day. Good, bad or otherwise.'

Michael smiled slightly. 'And where does Auden fall then? Good or bad?'

'Oh, that's easy,' said Clive. 'Have you seen *Four Weddings*? Popular film over here and in the States, I believe. Auden's poetry worked beautifully in that. His words are good. I don't know what *theory* they'd fall into, but they certainly *meant* something at the box office.'

Michael smiled: '*Let aeroplanes circle moaning overhead, Scribbling on the sky the message He Is Dead*. Right. So words that *sell* are good words?' said Michael. 'Good words *sell*?'

'Good words *mean*. And if they mean, they sell.' Clive was tired, irritated at himself for playing the uneducated, London sales guy to this pretentious Yank. It irritated him that he still felt a need to 'prove' himself, even to a tosser like Michael. But it was the inheritance the Orphanage had given him. As he'd grown older, there'd been fewer and fewer takers for a boy with 'attitude problems', and the adoption agencies were not keen to risk his placement and the mountain of paperwork that went with it. As soon as he turned 16, he was thrown out of care, and found himself in a succession of hostels and short-term, menial jobs. The experience had dented his confidence as much as it had forged it.

'Words that sell,' smiled Michael, sensing Clive's irritation. 'Good words are words that sell. Well now you've got *me* on the defensive. That's your business isn't it? Advertising?'

Clive didn't smile. 'A part of my business, yes. But you've got to remember, Michael, the words we use, the words I write, reach a global audience. It's all very well looking at a poem that, maybe half a dozen people know and creating a global theory of linguistics. But once you've sent a message to the world and the world *gets* it... then you don't *need* your theory. You've found the right words.'

Michael laughed quietly and finished his drink. 'Sure. It's easy. I wish I had your certainty.' Bella sniffed cautiously at his shoes, as he leaned forward and poured the last of the wine into his glass.

Clive started to reply. 'It's a certainty based on experience... *real* life - '

Nicole called from the kitchen.

'Hon'? Can you give me a hand?'

Over a dinner of goulash, macaroni and salad, Nic and Michael talked a lot about his work, the courses he taught and the pressure his publisher was putting him under to write another book.

'I've got no idea what it's going to be about, but I'd like to do something a little different this time. In fact, something Clive said earlier really inspired me. Imagine,' he looked to

Clive, with an exaggerated wink '... a book on the linguistics of advertising?'

'Can I get anyone coffee?' Clive pushed back his chair and began clearing dishes.

'Oh, thanks, yes,' said Michael. 'But Nicola, what about your work? I don't understand why it's taking so long to track our Elizabeth down? They've been keeping records in this country for hundreds of years, surely - '

'No, not *surely*!' Nicole was expansive and rather drunk, flushed in the low lighting. 'I've found a birth record – I'm pretty sure it's Elizabeth's. But you mustn't think such records were a given in those days... parents often lost children in the first few weeks or months, and baptisms cost money, so many didn't bother registering their children until they were sure they were strong enough to survive. And then maybe, after a few months, they simply forgot.

As for death records – there's nothing in Derbyshire, where she was born. But we don't know what her name was when she died.

And I told you, didn't I, that the records show her sailing for the US? Yes, she went off to marry someone. She may well have died there...'

Michael smiled. 'Hmmmm, she's such an interesting case – '

'Yes. I wonder if she *did* marry the guy she went to? I imagine she'd have had little choice – her family were very proud of her leaving for the 'new world' – they put it in the Parish newsletter. It would have been hard to turn tail and come back to the UK.'

Clive poured coffee and sat back in his chair. 'Maybe she did neither? Maybe she used the opportunity – the free ticket – to disappear.... went out to the Wild West.'

Nicole laughed. 'Yeah, maybe you're right. The poems are all quite dark – quite a few about death and disappearance... none about cowboys, though!'

They laughed.

'So,' said Michael. 'What's the next step?'

'Well, I've written to Alma....' She looked to Clive. 'She's an amazing researcher we knew in Cali. I was hoping she'd have an idea as to how we could track Elizabeth. At worst, she'll be able to give me some context – what would it have been like for a young woman at that time? Was it commonplace for young English women to emigrate?'

'Alma's definitely the woman for the job...' nodded Michael. 'But I got the impression the book was about the poetry, rather than the history?'

'Sure, sure. It still is... but I need the context for the poems. I call them poems, but they're more fragments.'

'Yes, I remember they were more like notes – from a workbook? Remember the piece about leaving? Ummm...

And even as I see you go,
I see nothing,

but that you must, therefore, return.
All things being even.

All things on balance . . .

They're nothing but fragments, really.' Michael threw back another glass of wine.

Nic blushed and quickly looked to Clive who was staring intently at Michael.

'Oh, don't get me wrong,' Michael said quickly, 'I think they had real potential... but it's very frustrating to see them incomplete...'

Nicole felt a stab of self-doubt. 'Well, I want to pull all of the fragments together. Edit them into complete pieces... it's a bit of a liberty, but... I don't know. I feel as though I *know* her... Understanding her life gets me closer to her. To the poems. Do you know what I mean?' She reached for her wine, shocked at this new idea.

Michael sat back in his chair with a dramatic flourish. 'What? You're going to *finish* the poems?'

Clive lit a cigarette. 'I think it's a great idea. It'll give your book a real edge – what did Cyn say? "It'll be like getting letters from a missing person." Even if you don't really *find* her – you might *discover* her in the poems. I can't think of anyone more able to put Elizabeth together.'

Nicole smiled, amazed at how easily he understood what she was doing. She reached out and squeezed his hand.

'Well,' Michael smiled at her indulgently. 'I'm sure it will be beautiful when it's finished. And don't forget – when it does hit the best-seller list – I'm owed a percentage.'

'What?' she laughed. 'How do you figure that?'

'It was my five bucks that bought Elizabeth's book!'

Nicole laughed and turned to Clive to explain. 'We went down to the flea markets every Sunday afternoon. I fell in love with a Deco lamp sticking out the top of this box of junk, but because it was getting late and he wanted to go home, the seller made us take the whole box!'

'God,' smiled Michael. 'Those Sunday markets were fun.'

Clive stubbed out his half-smoked cigarette and looked at his watch. 'Can I get you another coffee, Michael?'

'Oh, no, thanks. I'm very sorry. I didn't realise it was so late. Clive, forgive me, you must be exhausted after your flight and all.' He stood up.

'Nicola, it's been a wonderful evening. I can't begin to tell you how wonderful.'

He moved toward her and they embraced.

Nicole turned to Clive. 'Honey, shall we call a cab for Michael?'

'He'd be better off walking down to the tube – you'll flag one there much quicker than if we phone. They tend to hover just after the tube's closed.'

'Oh yeah – that'll be fine. So, Nicola, I'll call you about next week. Clive, it's been a pleasure. Thank you.'

Clive was clearing the table when Nicole came in from seeing Michael off.

'That was fun?' she ventured.

'Sure.'

'You know he's looking a lot older than last time I saw him.'

'When *was* that?' asked Clive, blowing out the last low-burning candle.

'Ummmm… about three years ago? Can't remember. It was a while after I came back from the States.'

'You mean the year after you left him in the States?'

'Yeah – he came over here just after that.'

'Did he?'

'Yes – I told you – he followed me – hoped we could work something out. But we couldn't.' She cleared the salad bowl from the table.

'No, I don't think you did tell me… You know, I'd never figured you two to have been that serious… I mean serious enough for him to follow you. You always make it sound like quite a casual affair.'

'Well, it was – well, it wasn't serious like you and me. I was young – younger. He was the head of the Lit Department. It was nothing serious…'

'Serious enough for him to follow you to try and sort things out, though.'

'Oh, Clive, honey, what is this? Are we going to get into ex-partners now? I thought we'd gone through this a long time ago? Shall we talk about Virginia, too? Don't get me started, please! I'm very drunk and very tired. So are you. We'll talk in the morning. Are you OK?'

She placed her hand gently on the side of his face.

'I'm fine.' He kissed her mouth, and gathered her hair at the nape of her neck, swaying her head from side to side. 'Just a bit rattled by this Feldmann's thing, and bloody Palmer. Seems he's been looking over the budget proposals I submitted… of course, he went straight to James with it.'

'What? How could he do that without talking to you first? It's your account.' Nic asked.

'I'm trying to get James to be a bit clearer about that,' he sighed. 'But anyway, Palmer tends to do what he wants. You can be sure he's over-inflated the numbers. I'll have to take the budgets back to Feldmann's if Paris have approved them. I'll look like a right idiot – or a liar.'

'Why should this bloke care what figures you've agreed with Feldmann's?'

'His bonus is based on income – he'll inflate the figure, grab his bonus, and – if the account doesn't bring in what he promised…. He'll blame me.'

'Jesus! What a nasty piece of work,' she sighed. 'Anything you can do to protect yourself?'

'Oh…. It may not turn out that bad. I've just got to focus on this New York meeting. We'll handle the numbers after we seal the deal. Maybe Feldmann's will be ok about paying more – maybe they'll stand their ground and AdVerbe will have to stick to the original offer. Either way, it's me, not Palmer, who will look like they've fucked up.'

'Isn't he the one who was sued for harassment? That sales girl….'

'Yeah. Cost the company a bomb. Rumour at the time said he should have gone with 'impotence' as his defence.'

'What?' she laughed.

'Word is he can't get it up. He's completely pissed most of the time.'

They laughed together, and he kissed her full on the mouth. 'I'm gonna miss you over the next few days.'

'What time's the flight tomorrow?' she whispered.

'Early.'

'Are you excited about seeing the boys?'

'Yeah. Nervous, too.'

'Sure. Don't worry. I know they'll be so happy to see you. Don't know about Virginia, but hey...'

'Well. We'll see. Go to bed. I'll be up in a minute.'

He finished loading the dishwasher and topped up the cat's water bowl. He lit a cigarette, and stared out into the garden.

He did not like Michael Forester – there was something fake about him; something 'unsaid'. Like Palmer. Damn it. Where was Palmer getting his information from? How had he seen the budgets so early? Clive knew Marina well enough to know she would not have undermined him – particularly not with Palmer whom she despised. He'd emailed her yesterday to see if she had any ideas, but she hadn't come back to him yet.

He felt uneasy and anxious, he wanted to do something, to fix something – but it was late, and Michael Forester and Palmer would have to wait. For now, he needed sleep and he needed to be ready for New York, for Feldmann's, for his sons.

He left Bella curled up on the lounge, and picked up Nic's notebook from the side table.

And in the hidden parts of my days
you'll find the moments when I imagined you,
prophesied you, knowing that
even then
I was already leaving you behind.

He switched off the lamp.

CHAPTER 10

It was after midnight when Marina Merriland shut down her laptop. She was cross-legged on the sofa, CNN was on the tv, providing some 'comfort' noise. She wasn't normally spooked staying at her cottage, but last night she'd been sure she heard something at the garage side of the house. She'd gone to check the exterior window was bolted, and then she'd double locked the interior door, and set the alarm. She would have liked to have a dog, but between her long hours, and the occasional nights she spent in London with her married lover, there wasn't a chance.

She stretched her arms, yawned and thought she should go to bed. She knew she should email Clive Alwynn – like her, he was smelling some kind of rat with the Feldmann's budget proposal. It wasn't just the discrepancies between the budgets Clive had submitted and the budgets that went to Paris; Clive's email said he'd suspected the numbers had been upped to ensure 'that certain people got bonuses'. Of course he was referring to Palmer. But for Marina, it was the fact that she couldn't trace *how* those changes had happened; *who* had changed the numbers that kept her awake tonight.

When Paris had called for her final sign-off, she told them she'd need a day or two to verify, but it was only when she accessed the system and found that the history of the submission – the date, time and approval of the files - had been deleted, that she started to panic.

This was not the first time someone had accessed the system and manipulated records. She remembered the Carlox account last year – she'd signed off budgets based on a forecast of 1.5 million Euros. The actual forecast that went to Paris was 2.5

million Euros. The account had reached only 1.5 million, yet several large bonuses were paid out to the account leaders – Palmer included. When Marina had gone into the system to figure out where the mistakes were happening, she'd been appalled to see that the account history had been 'lost'.

She rubbed her eyes and yawned loudly. 'OK,' she said. 'I give in!' But she knew she'd have to take a sleeping tablet if she hoped to shut down her brain tonight.

'Right,' she thought as she brushed her teeth. 'We've got London submitting over-inflated forecasts. But we've also got London receiving bonuses for meeting targets that they don't actually meet. How? And why were they getting away with it?' She needed to talk to IT. She needed to find out why these crucial records were being 'lost'.

She lay back in bed, waiting for the sleeping pill to kick in. There were only five people who were senior enough to access the system at a level where they could delete histories, and Palmer wasn't one of them. She turned off the lamp and drifted off, making a mental note to email Clive tomorrow. Something was up; and she was worried for him.

CHAPTER 11

Virginia was pleased with the scent of lamb ragout that greeted her as she opened the front door to the apartment. She'd wanted to leave work earlier, but the editorial meeting had dragged on, and now it was just after 6. She'd get the dessert sorted in a minute — just after she changed. Clive was due at 6.30.

'Hey Mrs Alwynn!' Rachel called from the kitchen. 'I'm just finishing up. I've got to pick up the boys from swim club.'

Virginia picked up the post and went down to the kitchen where Rachel was arranging a gorgeous vase of roses — white, yellow and the occasional pink.

'I'd say you had a nice dinner last night, Mrs Alwynn?' Rachel smiled knowingly.

'Oh!' Virginia blushed. 'It was nice, yes. Thanks again for looking after the boys — I hope I said so last night?'

'You did. Not a problem. Any time. As long as I'm home by 11, it's fine. Oh, I hope you don't mind, but I had a few minutes spare this afternoon, with the boys swimming and all, and I baked an apple crumble. Save you the trouble of dessert tonight.'

Virginia thanked Rachel warmly, silently cursing her efficiency.

'OK. I'll go get the boys. See you in about 10 minutes. Are you nervous about tonight?' she ventured.

'It's not a big deal, Rachel. The boys' father comes over occasionally...' and her words trailed away.

As Rachel shuffled her way down the hall, Virginia looked up from the mail she'd been blindly sorting and looked at the roses.

Oh my God! Matthew! She opened the small card attached to the stems: *'I'd put these in a really prominent place tonight, V. Let him know that other men are after you! Mx'* She blushed again and put her hand on her mouth to stifle a giggle. What on Earth was wrong with her? She poured a large glass of wine.

They'd met up after work, at a small Italian place. Clearly, he'd been there before, as every waiter seemed to know him. Virginia had been glad to make it an earlier meeting – that meant she could come straight from work, and so there was no need to 'dress' for the 'date'. As it turned out, it suited him, too, as he had his kids this week, and the sitter was only available until 10.

'Oh!' she'd said. 'I'm sorry to take you away from your kids – I could have been more flexible...'

Matthew laughed. An easy laugh, she thought. 'No! I have them every second week. Mattie Jnr is 6; Stephie is 4. They're asleep by 7.30. They'll hardly know I'm gone. And besides, this is the first time I've been out at night since Angie's dinner – the night we met.'

'How long have you been divorced?' she asked. 'If you don't mind me...'

'Two years. Oh, we started off calling it a 'separation', but it was obvious it was over. Marianne is nothing if not pragmatic – she divorced me. Irreconcilable differences, apparently.' He laughed that easy laugh again; she liked the creases at the corner of his eyes – like he'd had too much sun at some stage. And she liked the way his curly brown hair was a just a little too long, just brushing the collar of his business shirt.

'And is she with anyone else?'

'Sure. She's remarried. Fought me for the kids, but thankfully I have a good lawyer, and I only have to suffer the asshole she married once a fortnight – when I drop the kids off. Oh – excuse my French, as you Brits say.'

Virginia laughed, and he ordered more wine.

Over the next hour or so they laughed and shared so much about their pasts. Virginia found herself telling him about the loneliness, about Clive's emotional distance, the dreams she'd had, her boys and her ferocious desire to make their lives complete – even without their father.

By the time the taxi pulled up outside the apartment building and he walked her to her door, she was flushed and giddy with the wine, the great food and the cold air on her warmed cheeks.

When he leaned over to kiss her goodnight, she'd decided she'd let him. She decided she wanted to feel another man's mouth on hers – someone's other than Clive's. The kiss had sent a shiver through her, and had she lived alone she had no doubt she would have taken him upstairs.

But now, in the cold light of the next day, she suspected it would have been one night only. Matthew may have been charming and intelligent and sensitive, but she didn't *need* to see him again. She could survive without him.

The doorbell shattered her reverie. 'Shit'. Clive was here already. She hadn't had time to change or to do her hair – but she had fixed her make-up before she left the office, so it couldn't be too bad.

She took a deep breath, and opened the door. They paused for a second, taking in one another's faces.

'Hi,' she smiled slightly, opening the door wider. 'Come in.'

Clive handed her the flowers – a nondescript bunch of carnations he'd picked up at the grocery store down the road.

'Hi Ginnie.' He bent forward and kissed her awkwardly on the cheek. 'How are you?'

'Fine! A little nervous, actually!'

They laughed a little.

'Come through to the kitchen. Whiskey?'

Clive glanced about the apartment and felt a strange connection coupled with a jolting disconnection; objects looked strangely familiar – that painting, the photo on the hall table... Ginnie and her parents on holiday in Greece - like memories, but they were lost in the... *newness* of New York and this New York apartment. The apartment was not large, but Ginnie's natural sense of colour and balance had made the most of it. Everything was in its right place, adding an air of order. There was little colour – Ginnie was naturally drawn to pale woods, the Scandinavian end of the design scale. He smiled, remembering Nic's gradual invasion of the house – the odd bits and pieces of colour that appeared. Never clashing, but adding layers of warmth.

'How was the flight?' she asked, standing at the kitchen counter, looking to Matthew's roses, then to Clive's carnations, and back to Matthew's roses. She wasn't sure she owned another vase, and quickly grabbed a glass jug from the shelf.

'Nice roses...' he said, feeling a little awkward. 'Flight was fine. I got in last night – meetings all day. You know how it is.' They looked at each other suddenly, remembering *exactly* how it had been, then looked quickly away. She arranged the flowers, and poured him a whiskey.

In the bright light of the kitchen he could see she'd changed – aged a little, but changed, too. Her face was leaner, sharper – but it wasn't the look of weight-loss, even though she'd clearly embraced New York's obsession with gyms. No. Her face had taken on a harshness he'd not seen before.

'Where are the boys?'

She stirred the pot on the stove. 'Oh, they're at swim class. Rachel's picking them up – she's our part-time nanny. She's great. They won't be long.' She tapped the wooden spoon against the rim of the pot. 'They love swimming. There's a great pool just near the school – community, but we had to wait six months before we could register. Jack's actually on the swim team – one Saturday a month they do a gala thing.' She wished she could stop chattering. 'Let's go through to the lounge, this has got to simmer for a while.' She put the lid back on the saucepan.

'Lamb ragout?' he smiled. 'Great.'

The lounge curtains were drawn back.

'Wow,' said Clive. 'Quite a view!'

'Something's got to compensate for ten flights up with an unreliable elevator. Please, sit down.' She put the jug of carnations on the coffee table, and a large ball of long tortoise-shell, white and black fur leapt onto his lap, with a strange, broken *Meow!*

'Goodness! Hello puss!' He smiled. 'How's work then, Ginnie?'

She talked enthusiastically about her latest projects, and told him how she'd had to turn down the offer of promotion. 'It was impossible. I'd never be home before midnight. Not fair on the boys.' She hoped her point wasn't too obvious, but it was the truth: she was, to all intents and purposes a single mother, and the promotions and chances of change that Clive undoubtedly took for granted, were closed to her forever. 'No. Not fair on the boys....'

Clive turned to the window to hide a sudden rush of guilt. *The boys.* What would they make of him turning up in New York?

Ginny topped up his whiskey. 'How's *your* job going?'

He mentioned the Feldmann's account. 'Gosh!' She half-smiled. 'You'll be running the place next. How is Nicole?'

'Oh – she's fine, still working on the book.'

The front door flew open and the boys exploded into the hallway, Rachel, loaded up with school bags and coats, close behind.

'Jack! Ben! Slow down – Jack give it back to him!'

The fat cat leapt from Clive's lap, either running from the commotion, or maybe toward it.

'Mommy! Mommy!' They raced into the lounge room, their hair all fluffy and half-dried, laces undone. They skidded to a halt when they saw Clive; it was as if a film had frozen.

'Boys,' smiled Virginia encouragingly. 'Look who's come to see us.'

Rachel disappeared into the kitchen to unload the wet swim things into the dryer.

'Hi you two,' whispered Clive. He was flummoxed by a wave of emotion that threatened that choked his voice.

Ben looked from Virginia to Clive over and over again, confused. 'Mommy?'

'It's alright Ben,' smiled Clive. 'It's me – Daddy.'

The little boy's face broke into a huge, gap-toothed smile. 'Daddy! Daddy!' and he launched himself into Clive's arms.

'Hello little man!' Clive kissed his hair and breathed in the smell of him. He looked across the room to Jack.

'What about a hug, then, Jacko?'

Jack stared for a moment and then ran from the room, slamming his bedroom door shut.

Virginia jumped up. 'Sorry Clive – I'll go and talk to him.'

Rachel reappeared.

'Hi Mr Alwynn, I'm Rachel Prior.'

'Hello,' he said, looking past her to the hallway.

She was putting on her coat. 'Don't worry too much about Jack,' she smiled. 'He's a great kid – everyone loves him – always invited to birthday parties. Smart, too. Oh, and he swims good. He's just a little messed up. Anyway, it was lovely to meet you.' She closed the front door behind her.

Ben climbed down from Clive's arms. 'Do you want to see my cat?'

Clive nodded.

'His name's Porkie. We found him in the bin. He's usually in the kitchen.'

Clive followed behind and gave the ragout a stir.

Virginia looked flustered when she reappeared. 'Sorry about that – he doesn't want to come out. He's a little upset.'

'But he'll have to come out – I only have tonight.'

'I know that,' she said quickly, taking the spoon from him. 'But if he doesn't *want* to …'

'Well, he'll bloody well have to!'

'Oh Clive – don't start. For Christ's sake! They haven't seen you for two years!'

'And whose fault is that?' he hissed.

Ben stood frozen to the spot, struggling to hold the huge cat, looking from Clive to Virginia fearfully.

'Oh, Ben,' Virginia shot a warning glance at Clive, and hurried to stroke Ben's hair. 'Introduce Daddy to Mr Porkie!'

The boy hesitated for a moment. 'Here's Mr Porkie, Daddy! He's fat!'

Clive stroked the cat's head – 'Delighted to meet you, Mr Porkie! You are so fat!'

Ben giggled with delight.

'Daddy? Do you remember that cat called Sebastian?'

Jack appeared in the kitchen doorway. 'Of course he remembers Sebastian, you idiot. He lives with him.'

CHAPTER 12

Rachel Procter rode the Subway a few stops home. The elevator clunked and ground its way up to the 12th floor. The hall lights were low – energy-saving light bulbs that made the fading paint an even more jaundiced yellow.

She pulled the bunch of keys on a chain from the top pocket of her coat, and undid all six locks. Her parrot shouted out from the cage in the corner.

'What time do you call this?' he screeched in Hebrew.

'Oh, Menashe. It's just gone 7. I'm allowed to stay out until 11. That's what we agreed, remember? How was your day?'

'Tardiness is not an attractive quality.' He cawed again.

She laughed and booted up her computer. 'Come on, out you come.' She opened the door of the cage and he strode out onto the desk indignantly. 'Do you want the t.v on?' She flicked through the channels until she got to the Shopping Channel. 'There you go, boy. Ooooh, look: lovely jewellery.'

'Lovely things!' he cried delightedly, bobbing up and down. 'Lovely things!'

She went through to the kitchen and stirred the Crock-Pot. She had another chapter of her book to finish tonight. First, she had to phone her mother. She sighed, poured a small glass of sweet wine, and braced herself for the weekly update of how well her sister was doing, how she was expecting again, how her husband was starting his own dental practice, how her brother's wife had invited Rachel over for Sabbath (an invitation she consistently declined)... And, then, the inevitable closing question. 'And you, Rachel? How are things?' Her mother tried hard not to sound disappointed, but even her question was weighed down with the sad knowledge that her eldest daughter was an overweight spinster living in a tiny apartment and looking after another woman's children.

After the call, she'd have a quick shower and settle in for a long night of writing. Aside from Menashe, she had few friends but the characters of her novel. She was writing a romance and she knew she put off finishing it. She was half certain that she'd never publish it, but it was a good excuse not to attend dinner parties, or gatherings, and it provided a plausible answer to questions 'What do you do?' Or 'Why aren't you married yet?'

And then of course she had the boys. She loved them. She really did. Their mother didn't realise how lucky she was. Imagine leaving their children's father and taking them halfway around the world? She saw the letters and cards he sent to his boys – Rachel saw everything – but she guessed that Virginia withheld them from the boys. She heard Clive's messages on the ansaphone, and was sure that Virginia didn't pass them on to his sons.

The boys were the core of Rachel's days; often the only people she met. They relied on her, shared secrets with her. They kept her going.

Right. She hit the speed dial, while Menashe picked at her pretzels with his long claws. 'Hi Mommy, it's me.'

CHAPTER 13

Gustav poured another whiskey. 'And that's how I see things, put simply. Another, Clive?'

Clive nodded. It was late Wednesday evening, and Clive and Gustav had eaten at a little bistro about ten minutes walk away. Gustav's New York penthouse overlooked Central Park, and was close to Clive's hotel, so they'd decided on a nightcap; an hour had already passed.

'I truly believe,' Gustav continued, 'we are all quite powerless, in terms of outcomes.'

'And this is something you *learned* over time – thanks,' he took the glass from Gustav.

'Yes – whether I wanted to or not. I had no choice. Life taught me.'

'Life's lessons. Yes. I've heard about those,' he smiled. 'So you think all of us have to face up to those lessons. What if one chose not to – '

'Choice is an illusion, my friend. We don't choose the path, we don't choose the lessons that will come before us, and we don't choose whether or not we learn. We simply continue along.....'

Clive laughed gently. 'Surely not. What about all those times we arrive at crossroads – life-changing moments when we have to choose one of two options? Say – I don't know – say you're offered a job in Tokyo, but that will mean turning down a job in New York. You choose Tokyo and meet your future wife there.'

Gustav smiled. 'I know where you're going with this: you believe there's a possibility that there's a woman in Manhattan who may have been your wife had you taken the Manhattan job?'

'Sure. If you'd have chosen New York, how different would your life have been?'

'Ah,' said Gustav. 'We're back to choice again. But you see, Clive, you didn't choose Tokyo. You only think you did. That's one of life's great tricks: to make us feel as though we're in charge. As if *we're* navigating our way.'

'So who's guiding us, then? God?'

'Goodness, no. God is simply an excuse – a way to rationalise when life throws up one of its surprises. Listen – you may have a wife in Tokyo, but on a business trip to the States, you meet and fall in love with a beautiful woman who lives in Manhattan. "*If only you'd taken the job in New York!*" you cry. "*Then you would have met her earlier, and would now be married to her! God is cruel*".... and you take the American for your mistress without guilt.'

Clive laughed and downed his drink. 'Well then, in that case I've chosen to have both of them.'

'Hmmmmm,' Gustav smiled, swirling the remaining whiskey in his glass. 'Or maybe you think you've chosen not to choose between them? At any length, according to your theory, both women had *also* made choices which led them to this point.

Are you sure that Ms Manhattan would settle for being only your mistress?'

'Ha! Well, maybe. Maybe she'd make *bad* choices!'

They laughed.

'No, my friend,' sighed Gustav. 'You start your journey here,' he jabbed his finger into the air. 'And you finish over there. Along the way, experience happens.'

'Jesus, Gustav, that sounds rather bleak. Meaningless.'

'Ahhhh. Now he wants *meaning*,' Gustav laughed, flushed with the whiskey. 'I don't *know* what it means, Clive, but I know it's not meaningless. I do feel as though I am part of something larger, something beyond me. But it's not about God – I was raised to call it God, but I think it's more about the way our lives unfold. I have a sense of continuation, of a chain of which I am but one link... my grandfather, my father.... Do you not feel that connection with your father, Clive? With your sons?'

Clive sighed and ran his hand through his hair. 'No. I don't think I do, Gustav.' And he felt a dull sadness, thinking back on last night's disastrous meeting with his boys. 'At any length, I have to get going – we have an early start tomorrow – '

'Yes,' said Gustav, roused from his thoughts. 'I didn't realise how late it was – yes. I'm sure our colleagues are already sleeping! My brother Walter is arriving tomorrow morning. Sadly, Alonso is too frail to travel, but he may join the video conference.'

'Video conf?' Clive frowned.

'Yes, your boss, James McKinnie, has asked to join the meeting? His office called this afternoon. They said you had recommended he attend?'

'Oh.' Clive was confused. 'Oh, yes, of course,' he said, hiding his surprise. 'Gustav – thanks for your hospitality. I'll see you tomorrow.'

They shook hands warmly, and Clive threw on his coat.

'I'm sure the new ideas will sail through, Clive. I like your idea of a three-phase campaign - starting at now, and working our way back to our beginnings. And that gives us room to…. well, maybe to change things later.

Walter will be in a hurry to get back to Manila – and it doesn't matter what the others think, to be totally honest. The Board and the Exec only have power of veto over financial matters.'

He nodded to Clive as the elevator closed.

Staring out across the New York skyline, Gustav thought about Clive. Imagine, he thought, not feeling the reassurance of the past at your back. How could the man not feel that connection with his father? Perhaps even worse, why did his sons not provide him with a sense of the future reaching back to embrace him? How did Clive Alwynn survive each day without that sense of hands reaching out to him across time?

Even now, he felt Alonso, his brother, slipping away... certainly Walter had let go – at least on a moral level - a long time ago. The thought of Walter made him sad and angry. Gustav had held tightly, perhaps too tightly, to the hand of his own son, and when the boy died, it seemed that Gustav had been flung headlong into a dreadful emptiness.

But gradually, over the years, he'd realised that death hadn't erased the boy. Lilli had helped him to see this. Talking with her late into the evenings, telling stories of the boy, had helped him to reach out into the darkness and grasp, once again, the pale, small hand he feared had been lost forever.

CHAPTER 14

Alex Palmer was working late. It was 6pm. The team had decamped to the pub, and Esther had already texted three times. He was due at her parents at 7. He texted back with his standard message. 'Crisis here. Leaving as soon as I can...unlikely I'll be able to make it, darling. X.' If there was a downside to marrying money it was that the bitch felt as though she owned him.

He was going through the final changes he'd ordered on the creative boards for tomorrow's vid conference. He'd arranged to meet with Walter Feldmann at 8; Feldmann didn't have long – he was flying to New York tonight in time for tomorrow's Board meeting. Palmer wanted to give him a new copy of the presentation. Like Palmer, Walter thought Alwynn's ideas were crap. Well, he hadn't said so, but Palmer sensed a reticence that he was quick to exploit.

So, as soon as Clive had flown to New York, Palmer popped into James' office to voice his concerns.

'It's a bit awkward, James, particularly after our meeting with Clive, but he does seem to have taken too much on - only to be expected with all this new responsibility. I've tried to reach him on the mobile – probably better if we join them by vid. conf. and give him some support? Just to be sure he's got it right. I mean he's already undercut us budgets-wise... If we stand any chance at all of clawing the money back...'

James' boredom and irritation had made it easy.

'And I have to say,' Palmer said gravely, 'not *all* of the Feldmann brothers are so taken with Clive's direction. I spoke with Walter – the youngest one – yesterday and he's got very strong ideas on the direction we should take. He's quite a creative chap – uses his money to make films, would you believe. But he's going to be much easier to work with – and he understands he has to put money into this project if he wants it to really work for the bank.'

So, now he finished uploading the revised presentation to Walter Feldmann's extranet. One of Feldmann's secretaries was on standby in New York, ready to overwrite the presentation Clive had sent to the bank earlier, and to print and bind Palmer's new proposals, ready for distribution at tomorrow's presentation. He chuckled to himself.

Deborah looked up from her computer.

'Working late, Debs?' he smiled falsely.

'No – well, yes…'

'You should be careful, darling. Burnout is a common ailment in Sales. How have things been going with the Feldmann's gig?'

'Well, it's only my second week on the account, but I reckon I'm getting there.'

He looked at her breasts and thought that even though short plump girls *might* be attractive, they tended to be a bit more desperate; a little too clingy. And the Lord knew this one had been clingy. But she still had the hots for him, and he wouldn't mind another go at those huge tits.

He walked over to her desk, as she hurriedly shut down her internet search.

He looked around the office, checking there was no one there, and reached into her bra, and squeezed her breast viciously.

'Get off me, you arsehole!' And she pushed him away, tearing her shirt. He imagined her face in his lap, and lunged toward her. 'Come on Debs…. You don't want to upset the boss, do you?'

The phone on his desk rang. He cursed and snatched it from its cradle.

'Yes James…. no, don't worry! I'm working on it as we speak… It's all set. Vid Conf at 4pm. Yes, I'll drop Alwynn a line tonight. Ok. Good! See you tomorrow.'

He smiled at Debs who was quickly packing away her laptop and shoving her things into her bag.

'Oh, Debs. I'm afraid we'll have to put this off. I'm far too busy.'

Debs hurried to the elevator and pressed the call button frantically.

'Incidentally,' he said, leaning against the still closed doors. 'I spoke with the team today. I'm afraid the lads don't have a lot of confidence in you. Time to buckle down. Maybe you should give the pub a miss tonight.'

'You're an arsehole, Palmer. You always were. If you ever come near me again, I'll have you up for harassment. The company won't bail you out twice.'

He laughed contemptuously. 'Oh Debs. You disappoint me. Everyone on the team knows you threw yourself at me. They all know your fat little arse has been in my bed more than a few times. How do you think that will go down at a Tribunal?'

The elevator doors opened and she hurried inside. She didn't cry until the doors closed.

Palmer forgot about her immediately, gathered his things and took a cab to Feldmann's hotel – he'd be early, but that would mean time for a quick drink before the meeting. Walter Feldmann was 10 minutes late, so Palmer had time for two drinks.

'Mr Palmer!' The banker reached out his hand.

'Mr Feldmann! Please – call me Alex Lovely to see you. Please, sit down! Barman? What will you have, sir?'

'Oh – Champagne. Yes, I think Champagne.' Palmer instructed the barman to bring him the best, and noticed that the bar had gone suddenly silent as a young Asian girl dressed in a very short skirt, stilettos, and a very low-cut top tippy-toed her way across the room.

'Wally!' she cried. 'Why didn't you wait?'

'Because, my darling, you take an inordinate amount of time to dress in such a small amount of clothing.'

Palmer rose to his feet, quickly appraising the childish, small breasts. 'Mrs Feldmann. What a pleasure to see you.'

The girl giggled loudly, stifling a snort with her hand.

Walter looked annoyed. 'No, Palmer. This is Corrie. My secretary.' The girl giggled even more loudly.

'Shut up,' snapped Walter. 'Here. Drink this and just be quiet.' He pushed a glass of Champagne toward her.

'Well,' Palmer shifted uncomfortably. 'I'm so glad we could meet before tomorrow's meeting, Mr Feldmann....'

'It's in my interest, Palmer. About this Clive Alwynn: you say he's no longer on the account?'

'No. We've moved him off... Well, we're about to.'

'Good. He was much too close to my brother, and I cannot have Gustav interfering with our plans any longer. He is holding our progress back.'

'Well, after tomorrow, Alwynn will definitely be off the account.'

Walter signalled for a waiter to top up his glass. 'After the meeting, I will be in charge, and the first thing I want to talk about is your plan for our website. You mentioned some designs, and some sponsorships?'

'Yes! I have some layouts here....' Palmer could hardly contain his excitement. He would make this account bigger than

Alwynn could ever have imagined. 'I think you'll agree this font works so well, and the palette we've chosen reflects......'

'No.' said Walter flicking through the pages dismissively. 'We're going to have make them more appealing. Have you thought about a pretty face to welcome our customers?' He gestured toward Corrie who giggled loudly. 'The smile of a beautiful girl induces such calm – and our clients need to feel calm if they are to give us their money!' Corrie was, by now, in silent paroxysms of laughter, and Walter smiled at her indulgently.

'And tell me more about this sponsorship plan? Are you still promising to get third-party buy-in? If, as you said, we could get to a point where the website is funded by newer, lesser agencies riding on Feldmann's established reputation... '

'Oh,' stammered Palmer. 'Of course. My Sales team are well underway with it.'

'Good, because this is the only way we will continue to work together Palmer. Corrie, go and tell the Concierge to call our car to the front. We must get to the airport. Go away and think of the new look, Mr Palmer. I have several faces in mind.... I'll email some shots on my way to the airport. I expect tomorrow's presentation to include quite a few of them.'

Palmer stared open-mouthed. 'Um, right. Yes. I'll... um..... get on with that now.' And he rose unsteadily, gathering up the layouts.

As he walked away, Walter called after him. 'Oh, and Mr Palmer? We'll have to look at those ads again. I have some ideas for a shoot. Let's talk about that next time.'

Palmer nodded, and desperately dialled the Designer's number. It was going to be a long night.

CHAPTER 15

Michael stretched back into the sofa. He looked around the room. Nicola had always had eclectic taste, and he felt enveloped, comforted and disturbed by the signs of her. He remembered those black and white photos – the bleak snowy landscapes, bare trees reaching up into the grey sky; the frozen lakes; kids dancing about in a fountain, their wild movement blurring their forms into abstraction. He marvelled that she always undervalued her talent.

The cushion covers intrigued him, all one-offs with seemingly little relation to one another – one deep green, one a soft, coffee brown, another a delicate white lace where the cat slept, curled into a tight ball. He ran his finger along the side of his wine glass – she had such an eye for beautiful, odd things. She'd find them in second-hand stores, or markets and they'd blend together as if it was meant to be.

It unnerved him to see how easily Nicola's things – these pieces of her – changed and re-formed under the weight of Clive's presence. The photographs were arranged in the corner, in a stark, pale wood cabinet (Scandinavian, he thought, like the dining table). The floors were blonde wood, and Nicola's cushions rested comfortably and naturally in the uncompromising deep leather brown of the sofa.

Nicole hurried in, replacing the phone in its cradle. 'Sorry – Clive's office. They have his mobile number, I don't know why they don't use it.'

'He's quite important, then?'

'God yes. They never leave him alone. That was a guy called Palmer. He's a real drama queen. Always panicking. I must have given him Clive's mobile number six times already! He sounded smashed.... I hope he doesn't get through to Clive actually. He sounded quite threatening.... I don't know..... probably just the booze talking.....'

'How's Clive enjoying New York? Does he stay with his kids when he's there?'

'He hasn't been over for about two years. Just too much on and it's always a bit of struggle with the ex-wife.'

'Oh? Don't they get on?'

'No. She hasn't made it easy. When they decided to call it quits, that was it. She took the boys to New York, he stayed here, and they both got on with their own lives. Her lawyers really made his life hell. I get the feeling that when the legal stuff was over, he just had to walk away.'

'It must be nice to be able to do that – just walk away.'

Nicole blushed slightly. 'Well – yes, but that doesn't mean that it didn't hurt him.'

'Sure.'

'Anyway,' she hurried on. 'How's your time in London been? Come through to the kitchen and tell me while I sort out dinner.'

'Hope you didn't go to too much trouble...'

'Michael, come on,' she laughed. 'You know me and kitchens – whatever we're eating, it's wasn't a trouble!'

Over dinner, Nicole asked questions about his research and his teaching in the States – she hoped that they could stick to talking about the present, rather than the past. But it wasn't long before they were discussing mutual friends, restaurants they used to eat at, the creeper she'd planted at the side of the house.

Michael was halfway through an anecdote about one of their neighbours.

'... And you remember Claude's son used to visit? Really weird guy – fat wife and all those kids? Station wagon? Turns out Claude disinherited him – found out that every time they visited, the son would take a handful of Claude's first editions – you remember Claude had been a Classics professor? The son thought he was too senile to notice, but old Claude's still sharp as a pin.'

'Did he get the books back?'

'Some of them, but the son had already sold lots of them.'

'Jesus. Poor old Claude.'

'Yeah. Strangely enough, I reckon he's sorry they don't visit anymore. He's quite lonely.'

She was staring into her glass of wine.

'Nicola?'

'Oh – sorry. I was miles away.'

'Back in San Fran?' he smiled gently.

Nicole smiled. 'Sort of.'

'Nicola? Do you miss it?'

'No, not really – London is great. I mean, it has its problems, but – '

'I meant *that time* – do you miss the life we had?'

'Oh Michael – God – I – look...' She stood up and took their dinner plates to the kitchen. 'It was a long time ago – well, it feels a lifetime ago. My life is different now. I'm married to Clive and my life is here – with him.'

Michael stood up. 'But it was *good*, Nicola. What we had was *special*. God, this is coming out all wrong – it all sounds so trite.'

'Michael, please – '

He was on his feet now, the wine lighting up his pale features. She reached for the wine bottle – 'Gosh – we've finished this one. I'll go and ...'

He held her by the shoulders. 'Nicola! I have to understand! Tell me. You woke up one morning and decided – what? – that you didn't want that life anymore? You were bored? That you didn't love me?'

They stood there like that for a long moment.

'Michael... ' Nicole moved away.

'Nicola – I'm sorry. I just need to get some.... some closure ...'
He slumped down into his chair. 'These last years have been
hell. I need to know...' He covered his face with his hands and
sighed. 'I'm sorry. I didn't want it to be like this – I guess I
was just so tense. The wine...'

'Oh, Michael.' She wanted to comfort him, to somehow undo
the last few moments and go back to talking about now. But
here they were – exactly where they'd been all those years
ago. She couldn't move forward to comfort him and she
couldn't walk away from the car crash of their relationship.
'Michael – I can't do this - '

'For God's sake, Nicola!' He stood up again, and she stepped
back. 'All I'm asking for is a fucking explanation, then I can
get on with my life and not wake up every morning wondering
'what if?' '

'Michael, I can't... I don't know how to...' She looked around
the room, grasping for some help from the world Clive and
she had built. She stopped at the photo on the bookcase. It
was a faded black and white snapshot of a young boy, maybe
seven years old, standing with his proudly beaming parents on
a sunny, windy pier. The boy held his stuffed toy to the
camera – a win in the shooting gallery perhaps.

A long time seemed to pass. Michael sighed again. 'I should
go.'

Even as he wrapped his coat him and walked out the front door, she refused to look away from that snapshot of a happy Sunday. She could almost hear the gulls wheeling overhead.

The first night she'd slept with Clive – the night they met at Giles' book launch – she'd crept out of bed in the early morning to find the bathroom. On her way back, she'd noticed the photo, illuminated by a streetlight shining through a gap in the curtains.

Clive found her there in the half-light.

'Southend Pier,' he whispered.

'Oh, sorry – it's a lovely shot. It's you, yeah?'

'Yes, I ...' He looked into her eyes and seemed to be searching for something. He hesitated for a long moment. 'No. I found the picture in a charity shop when I was about 16. I remember thinking how that could be me and my mum and dad. How happy they all looked......'

'I don't understand...'

'I was raised in care – never knew my parents. I was sorry for myself for a long time, went off the rails – until I found that picture. I found a history. Then everything seemed to go right. I got into college, got a job, got a life.'

'Wow,' whispered Nicole sleepily.

'Come on, let's go back to bed,' he said, and the desire for him was so strong she felt afraid, and as vulnerable and as joyous as that little boy on the pier.

The phone rang, and she turned away from the photo.

'Hello?' she mumbled.

'Hey, honey. Did I wake you?'

'Oh, Clive. How are you, my love? What time is it there? God, isn't the presentation today?'

Clive laughed. 'I *did* wake you up! Don't worry, it's after midnight here. I just got back from dinner with Gustav – the presso's in eight hours time.'

'How's Gustav?'

'Drunk, but then aren't we all? No, we had a great evening, actually. I really like him.'

'Yeah? So what did you talk about? The presentation?'

'No, we got quite philosophical really. Dunno – I'm finding it a bit disturbing now,' he laughed uncomfortably.

'Hey? Are you ok? What did he say?'

'Oh, just that we all imagine we're in control of our destinies, but we're not. Ha! Don't worry, babe, it's just the drink talking. How was Michael?'

'Oh – you know...' she sunk down onto the lounge. 'Just the same. Hey, are you nervous about the presso?'

'No – but something strange.... Gustav told me that James was joining the call via video conf.'

'What? You didn't know?'

'No. Very odd. Anyway – I've got to get some sleep. I can't wait to see you tomorrow night.'

Clive drank a large glass of water and fell into bed, thinking about the conversation with Gustav, and wondering why it disturbed him. '*Do you not feel that connection with your father, Clive?*'

Fathers were not a big part of Clive's life. His first experience of paternal care was Stephan, a 50 year old, well-read man who worked with him in a factory in Essex just after Clive had been thrown out of the orphanage. Stephan's family had arrived from Yugoslavia when he was a child, and even though he'd been sent to work at an early age, he'd continued with his education at various adult education centres. He introduced Clive to one such centre, and soon Clive was graduating from high school, and then accepted on scholarship to university. He'd felt at the time he should do something meaningful, something to make sense of his years of abandonment – psychology, maybe, or social welfare? But in the end, he chose Communications and Media.

After he graduated, he'd taken a job as a salesman with a small publishing firm, set himself up in a flat in Marylebone, and, for the first time in his life, felt as though he was in charge of his own destiny. It was at this moment when he was finally letting go of his past that a letter had arrived from a child welfare agency.

The official brown envelope contained a long, handwritten letter from a woman called Mavis Alwynn. She introduced herself as 62 years-old, and the mother of three children, not counting Clive. He fell back onto the couch, and loosened his tie. She was now married to a man called Trevor, and she had six grandchildren. She told him how her kids had helped her to deal with the longing she'd felt for him ever since the officials had taken him from her arms, a few hours after he was born.

She told him his father was a successful businessman, but she had no idea where he was now. She'd met him while on holiday with her family at Butlins; he'd been there with his pregnant wife and their young daughter. She'd fallen for his charm and his promise to see her once they all went back to London. She'd called him several times as the panic inside her grew at the same rate as the baby she carried. His secretary grew tired of her pleading, and, in the end, hung up whenever Mavis rang.

Of course, her conservative parents were horrified, and with hardly enough to support his own children, her father insisted she put the baby up for adoption. And, so, that was that. She'd hoped he'd had a good life. She'd never told Trevor about her dark secret – he'd never have understood.

She went on to detail his cousins, his aunts, dates of deaths, marriages and births, but he couldn't read any more. He folded the letter back into the envelope and buried it deep in the folder where he kept tax forms and other papers, and forgot about it.

Months later, when he married Virginia, his mother was not present. Stephan happily played the role of Groom's family, and Giles was his best man. He felt, even more, as if something - or someone - was missing.

Reach for me –
here I am. Just after you take
the wrong turn,
I spin you by your shoulders – you
cannot feel me. I am nothing more than
invisible hands dancing about you like so many
butterfly touches of love.

CHAPTER 16

After Clive hung up, she shuffled to the kitchen for coffee. 'God,' she sighed. 'Michael.' She'd been crazy to meet him on her own – but she'd imagined there were rules, agreed rules, that they wouldn't bring up the past. Oh, of course they'd talk about restaurants and neighbours and mutual friends, but wasn't it understood that talking about the relationship was out of bounds? It was over, had been for a long time. She saw no reason to go over it again.

She'd never seen Michael so distraught. Why hadn't he moved on, like she had? And anyway, it had been over for a long time – even before she left. At least he was flying out of London tonight and she wouldn't have to deal with any more of his angst.

As she showered, the hot water running down her body, she leaned against the tiles and tried to drown out the memory of those last days in San Francisco.

She'd already packed by the time he got back from lecturing. At first he thought it was some kind of a joke.

'Nicola, for goodness sake. Let's not do histrionics tonight. I've got early classes tomorrow and a desk full of crap undergraduate analyses of *As I lay Dying* to grade. What's wrong this time?' He poured himself a large glass of wine.

'I told you, Michael. I'm going back to London.'

'Well, if you're expecting me to come with you, forget it. This is the busiest month of the year for me...'

'I don't want you to come with me, Michael. I'm leaving here and I'm leaving you.'

Things had not been right between them for months.

They'd first met at a post-graduate drinks do. She'd been accepted as an MA student – partial scholarship, with half-time teaching – in the Literature department. He was the newly appointed head of Linguistics.

In the weeks that followed, he'd pursued her relentlessly. In the months that followed they took long weekends away up the Californian coast and, often, down into Mexico. She couldn't quite believe it was *her* flying through the breezy Californian sunshine in a classic convertible, with the head of the Linguistics department, laughing, feeling beautiful and intelligent. He loved to ask her opinion on new writers and laughed when she debunked one of his theories of language. Michael promised her a life she would never have imagined for herself.

When he told her he loved her and asked her to move in with him, she found it remarkably easy to tell him she loved him, too, and over time she grew to believe that she really did.

But then it all began to unravel. She could not articulate why or when things had changed. It may have been that he came home later and later; that he continued to join his students in the Post-Graduates' bar even after she'd decided she'd had enough of pretentious chatter and opted to spend her evenings at home working on her thesis; it may have been that he was losing interest in her or that she felt as though the Californian Fall was leeching her youth from her. But, in the end, she knew she'd made a mistake.

Sometimes, she suspected that she had simply stopped loving him. But then she'd reason that she had never really loved Michael Forester, and she hated herself for the way she had grabbed at him and the imaginary security he'd offered.

Nicole shuddered. The hot water had run out. She was sobbing now. She wasn't sure why – a great pain was rising up inside here. She wished Clive was here. There was so much she wanted to tell him. She climbed back into bed, dreaming fitfully of that last evening in San Francisco.

'What do you mean it's over? What's all this about? For God's sake, Nicola, this is not the night. Look, have a drink and calm down. We'll talk about it tomorrow. I'm sorry – I can't do this tonight.'

He turned and slammed the study door behind him.

She curled up on the sofa, checking the flight times on her ticket. 11am – Michael would be teaching when the taxi arrived. Another wave of pain gripped her womb. The nurse at the clinic had warned her of the 'aftershocks'.

Of course, she thought, such a vicious act, ripping the child from its safety, deserved this retribution. She curled tightly into the foetal position, stifling her groans in the cushion.

She woke and held Clive's pillow in her arms, smelling the scent of him.

I need to know
there's a hand breaking the ice
should I fall through.

CHAPTER 17

The Communications Executive – an impossibly long-legged blonde, dressed in an immaculately fitted trouser suit – leaned across the Board table and repositioned the microphones. She was wearing a mobile phone headset and occasionally murmured orders to unseen technicians. Clive scrolled through his presentation.

Gustav sat in the corner, taking calls and signing forms for a seemingly endless line of assistants.

Walter shouted into his mobile phone and slammed it onto the table. He was overweight, dressed in a lightweight suit, beige over a lavender shirt, and he was sweating profusely, despite the frigid air-conditioning.

'So, Clive,' he shouted across the room. 'Gustav tells me you're the brains behind the 'connections' crap?'

The leggy blonde assistant didn't seem to hear the profanity as she crept under the table and pulled and stretched cables.

'Hello Walter – 'crap' seems a little harsh – '

'Oh, really? Seems to me I'm not the only one who thinks so.....'

'Ignore him, Clive,' Gustav handed his mobile to a young man in navy blue. 'Walter is an 'artist' – and I'd suggest that if he wants to make the flight to Manilla this afternoon, we should get on with the call and discuss his 'insights' at another time.'

Walter smiled – more of a teeth-baring. 'I'm serious, Gustav. I was talking to one of Clive's bosses – Mr Palmer – yesterday. He agrees that we need to be a bit more... explicit. Out with the old, in with the new. You know – brave new world and all that...'

The blonde assistant startled everyone to silence, shouting 'Two minutes, Gentlemen!'

By now the table was surrounded by short men in brown suits. An eager and efficient army of young people in navy blue suits and white, high collared shirts withdrew, taking their coffee pots with them.

Gustav leaned back in his chair – 'Over to you, Clive.'

The blonde, fired the remote control at the screen. 'Come in, London! Welcome!'

Clive turned to see James adjusting his jacket, not realising the link was live. 'What the fuck are we supposed to – ' he was struggling with a mic cord.

Palmer was to his right, and interrupted the outburst. 'Good afternoon, New York. How are you all?'

Clive felt a sudden sense of unease. Why was Palmer on the call? Why had he been speaking to Walter? He saw that Gustav was feeling the same. He pushed away his doubts and began his presentation.

'First of all, can I say how wonderful it is to be here today. The first day of our new relationship. I want to thank you all for taking the time to be here – I know some of you have had long flights...'

Gustav interrupted. 'I'm sorry to say that my brother, Alonso, is unable to join us. He is rather poorly.'

The old men gathered around the table made low, sympathetic noises.

Gustav hadn't told them the full story. Alonso had slipped into a coma overnight. There was little hope that he would survive the day. Gustav had told Clive when they met for coffee before the meeting. 'I suppose it is to be expected,' he sighed. 'but it's still so... unexpected.' He laughed quietly. 'We were talking about such surprises last night, non?'

Clive smiled sympathetically. 'Yes, we were.'

'I remember Alonso taking me out for a drive when I was just fourteen. He was just 21, but to me he was the most... heroic, almost... he drove an Alfa Romeo. I remember looking out of my bedroom window every evening around midnight. I would be dressed in my nightclothes – and I would wave to Alonso as he sped away. I imagined the glamorous parties he was attending, the beautiful women, the air heavy with their perfume ... music, champagne and lights!

And then, the day before my 14th birthday, he called me downstairs just before lunch and demanded that I drive him to the village. I was astounded – scared, excited – I didn't want to let him down, but I was frozen with fear.

"Come on!" he shouted. "Drive!" As you can imagine we spluttered our way along the drive for a while and then –

suddenly – it all came together. It felt as though me and the car and Alonso were one – a unified thing … We flew along the lane, birds exploding up from the roadside bushes! I remember him laughing, throwing his head back, his cheeks flushed from the cold air. I have never felt that way again, really…….'

He cleared his throat. 'Anyway, we must focus on today's meeting – forgive me, I am a little tired.'

Clive reached out and placed his hand over the old man's. 'Gustav, please don't apologise. I understand – maybe not exactly, but I understand.'

Gustav looked up and smiled. 'Yes. I believe you might.'

CHAPTER 18

'Well, how long *are* you going to be here?' Ruby Winston put one hand on her ample waist and tapped her foot silently.

'Oh, not long Ruby. I just need to look over last night's runs…' Marina smiled unconvincingly. 'Why?'

Ruby sighed. 'I have a temp downstairs and she's gonna need that desk.'

'Oh, sure…' Marina looked up from her screen. 'Promise. It won't be long. I'll send the temp up on my way out – so no need for you to hang around.' This time she didn't smile.

Ruby turned on her heel and sauntered back to her own desk.

Staff turnover in the accounts department was the lowest in the company, a fact that often surprised Marina. Stuck in the basement with no windows, the air was thick with the dull blue-grey glow of neons.

Marina flicked through screen after screen of figures. She couldn't access this data from her laptop. All she could do was request a printout of data relating to certain accounts. But the printouts were a simplified narrative of events – Marina needed another level of detail.

The numbers didn't interest her, she knew them almost by heart; she was looking at the user codes. Every transaction, every update to an account was marked by a username, a coded reference to one of the senior members of AdVerbe. Hers was MRL – for Merriland, followed by her unique payroll number: 3454. There was also the suffix that denoted her as a 'super user' with high-level access to the system. Of course, she wasn't a 'supreme user'; she assumed *that* group of five codes belonged to the suits in Paris – they were odd configurations, none of them matching any names in the staff directory. For security reasons, no one knew them.

She found the Feldmann's file. AWN: there was Clive's budget submission, two weeks ago. Yes, the date was right – just after the Feldmann's pitch. PLM – Palmer! She double clicked on the entry dated just five days ago. A pop-up message sounded loudly: 'Access denied.' She frowned; she was senior to Palmer, when it came to numbers – she should have had complete access to his files. She re-clicked. Ruby leaned over her from behind, her long, red acrylic nail tapped the return key. 'Looks like you're trying to access areas you shouldn't be ...'

Marina spun around. 'No... I'm not! I'm trying to access the narrative for Feldmann's. Any reason why Palmer's files are locked?'

Ruby frowned. 'Shouldn't be – at least not to you. Lord knows they usually are to me. Move over...' She entered her own password and a new datasheet opened up. 'What are you after him for anyway?'

'Oh,' Marina stuttered a little. 'I'm not after him, I just need to have another look at the numbers.'

Ruby was still frowning, entering access codes. 'What? The printout I gave you wasn't enough?'

Marina half smiled. 'Ok. You got me. I think someone's screwed up the numbers somewhere along the way...'

'Well it wasn't anyone in my department,' Ruby's eyes flashed darkly. 'So if you're here to find an arse to kick, save it!'

'I'm sure it wasn't! Just help me look at Palmer's numbers and we might be able to settle it without a fuss.'

Ruby sighed heavily. 'Ok. You know this isn't the first time Palmer's numbers have been second-guessed. There – I'm in. Hmmmm, that's strange....'

'What?' Marina leaned into the screen.

'Well, it's Palmer's data, but ... but it's been overwritten.'

'How can you tell? Why is it still showing Palmer's code?'

'I don't know… look – if it was Palmer's original numbers you wouldn't have this yellow highlighting…'

'How does that happen?'

'Well, normally, that's how we can see when the supreme users have been 'correcting' numbers. Usually, I'd get an alert that they'd made a change and I'd make sure the numbers added up – they don't always, specially after Paris has been on the vino – and then I ok it so they can go live.'

'So these haven't gone live?'

'That's what's strange… these are live and kickin' – see? There's been activity here over the last few days… the last few hours.'

'What's the code? Who's the supreme user?' Marina's heart was beating faster.

'Hold on, hold on…' Ruby turned to her. 'I shouldn't be discussing this with you. You just haven't got the seniority.'

'Oh, come on Ruby…. You know me. I just want to sort this out – make sure you guys are left in the clear.' And she tried to smile winningly.

'Hmmmm. Here's the code – ' she tapped her nail on the screen. 'Not that it will be any use to you. Even *I* don't know who they are. But don't you dare say it came from me.'

Marina memorised the code.

CHAPTER 19

The plane bounced down into Stansted at 5.15.

'Jesus!' said the fat American beside him. '*That's* turbulence!'

Clive smiled. 'Yeah.' He had no more energy for pleasantries than he'd had for the past seven hours. He felt embarrassed that he'd rejected all the guy's attempts at conversation and smiled apologetically. 'Welcome to London, I guess...' The American smiled unconvincingly.

In the taxi on the way back, he ran through the last few days in his mind – not in an organised, narrative way – just snapshots. Jack's rage, Ben's anxiety, Virginia's anger, Nicole's drunken message on his mobile.

'God.' He rested back in the taxi, wanting to enjoy the familiarity of the Holloway Road, but feeling strangely apprehensive.

And then there was the presentation. What the fuck did Palmer think he was doing? By the time Clive was halfway through his introduction, Palmer had taken over the call and Clive had realised with a shock that the printouts the leggy blonde had distributed were not the ones he'd signed off. Instead, they were slightly edited versions of the first campaign – sepia-toned clocks gave way to cold, blue shots of computers and endless numbers rushing across screens.

Gustav had looked up, bewildered and angry.

'But Clive, we... I .....'

'Don't worry, Gustav!' Walter sighed and pulled himself up on his feet. As I told you, Mr Palmer and I have reviewed Mr Alwyn's work and – ' he nodded to Clive – 'while I think it has merit, it has not embraced the true spirit of Feldmann's, nor the direction in which we should be taking the bank.'

At this point he stared pointedly at Gustav, before meeting the eye of each of the startled Board members, who quickly murmured their acquiescence, sensing the balance of power had just swung to the youngest brother.

'Yes,' Palmer's pixelated smile chimed in from the screen. 'Here at AdVerbe, we work as a team – James and I think Clive did a marvellous job, but we can't thank Walter enough for the insight he's given us to your amazing organisation. Without that, we would have been floundering.'

The Board members followed Palmer's lead, applauding softly.

Gustav rose from his seat and walked stiffly from the room. Clive sat through Palmer's presentation, imagining he was grinding his teeth to stumps.

Afterwards, James McKinnie had left a message on Clive's mobile: '*Palmer seems to have a real feel for the account, and I think you'll agree his presentation on the video conf was superbe. Let's talk about it?*'

And one of the sales girls had forwarded him an email – why was Palmer calling a team meeting at 9 tomorrow – an hour before Clive was due to arrive? Clive knew that Palmer was making his move.

He ran his hand through his hair.

Nic. He needed to see Nic.

It was *still* raining in London.

CHAPTER 20

Character was a difficult thing to measure, Jay Swift thought. I mean, a woman might be cheating on her husband, a husband might be cheating on his wife. A long-serving employee might have his fingers in the till. But was this really an indicator of 'character', or simply an occurrence? Something that happened with little or no relation to the essence of the man or woman? Why could we not say that a man was 'acting out of character' at those times he disappointed us, and so, logically, he was proving his good character?

He lay back on the bed and watched the young woman dressing, wiping the tears off her face, snot dribbling from her nose. He'd just paid her £50 for straight sex, but had, against her will, chosen sodomy. Of course, she'd demanded more money afterwards, and he'd slapped her face hard.

But you could not pretend that this small, isolated incident was any measure of his character. He smiled to himself. It was only the middle-classes who got caught up in such debates... and it was the sanctimonious middle-classes who paid his bills.

After she'd gone, he took a quick shower, gave the desk clerk a 5 pound tip to ensure he'd forget the girl's cries, and headed to McDonalds for lunch. He hated King's Cross, but he knew it was the place to buy desperate and voiceless women.

He had a long night ahead of him. He'd sent his client pictures as requested, but she wanted more. She wanted pictures of the house, pictures of them together, she wanted addresses, emails, phone numbers.

But Jay didn't mind. The more he got into this case, the more he saw how much money was up for grabs. What had started out as a simple 'watch and report' had turned into something much bigger.

He opened his backpack and pulled out the crumpled sheets. If the numbers on these printouts were anything to go by, someone was screwing this company bigtime... it didn't take a genius to see that the amount going in was a lot less than the amount being taken out, and yet the end number stayed resolutely in the black. Someone was fiddling the books. Jay knew it would not be profitable to him to alert the company, but there was profit to be made. He reread the printout of the email. There were five names on this list: five potential hits, as far as he was concerned.

He finished his burger and headed for the Underground.

CHAPTER 21

'It doesn't make sense!' Clive ran his hand through his hair.

'You're right!' said Marina, drawing her dressing gown around her. 'It doesn't, and that's exactly why I emailed you.'

'You emailed me?'

'Come in, Clive... what time is it anyway? Yes, I emailed you... I thought that's why you were here?'

Clive looked confused, then sheepish... 'Umm, no, I umm... I thought...'

Marina stepped back to let him pass. 'You thought I had something to do with those figures being leaked to Palmer?'

Clive sighed, and threw his bag into the hallway. 'Sorry Marina. It's after 11... I won't stay long... the driver's waiting, and my wife...'

Marina poured them a glass of whisky and gestured to the lounge. 'Sit down, Clive... we've got a lot to talk about.'

CHAPTER 22

He reached across her and turned on the bedside lamp. She curled more tightly against him, and made a small groan of protest.

'God-' she sat up fast. 'What time is it?'

'4.'

'Oh... was your flight delayed?'

He reached for his whiskey and told her brief details.

'So what do you think he'll say?'

'Who?'

'James. Surely he can't take you off the account...'

'Of course not. I imagine Palmer has been in his ear since I left. You know what James is like – easily panicked. No... I'm sure it's fixable. We've got bigger problems - '

He saw her confusion. 'Well, with Walter trying to take the reigns from Gustav. I could happily smack Palmer in the mouth, the little shit.'

'If I had a dollar for every time you said that...'

'Anyway – how was Michael? Did he get away OK?'

'What do you care?' She re-adjusted her dressing gown. 'I bet you couldn't wait to see the back of him.'

'Well… I didn't have a lot of time for him – no. My wife's ex-lover… No. Not a lot of time. I saw the roses in the kitchen bin….'

'Yes. I never liked yellow…' She reached for his glass and he felt uneasy, remembering the drunken phone message she left last night.

'Nic?'

'Hmmm?' She was pretending to be distracted.

'You left me a message the other night…'

'Did I?' He could see she was panicking, trying to remember just as the fog lifted. 'When?'

'Not *when*,' he said. '*What*… you mentioned 'the baby'…'

'Really?' She laughed nervously. 'God – I don't remember… pissed again – '

'Nic. You told me you'd 'lost the baby'?'

'Clive – look – ' she turned away, her eyes stinging with tears.

'Oh, Nic! No – don't cry. I know I said I didn't want any more, but, hey, it was an accident – and – if that's what you want – fine – I – I don't know what to say… maybe it was meant to be…'

'Clive – no – I… it wasn't yours…'

She watched the blood drain from his face as a hard frown replaced his confusion.

'Oh , no – ' she rushed forward to hold him. 'No – it's not like that!'

She didn't know whether to laugh or cry.

'Clive – I – I had an abortion when I was with Michael...'

'God – you didn't tell me...'

'No. Well. It's not something I ...'

'But you didn't tell me...'

'I know... I'm sorry... but really, it's... it's before you – it's before us...'

'But it's *you*, Nic. It's *you*. And you're mine and I can't imagine there's things you'd hold back...' He could feel the ground slipping away beneath him.

'Clive, baby...' She reached out to him. 'It's OK.'

She knew how he needed certainty. She knew how he needed to know her. The first months she'd told him about the redwoods, and the drive up the coast. Californian wines (terrible!) and the old man next door, all you can eat buffets, guns in every home, the bay, the Bridge... anything but the truth. She shuddered. No. What was the truth?

'For God's sake!' Clive snatched the glass from her hand. 'Answer me!'

'What?...' She tried to pull her wrist from his grip.

'Is that why you and Michael split up?'

She wanted to say 'No...' She wanted to tell him about Charlotte... and the humiliation. She wanted to explain that she'd never really loved Michael, to tell him about the loneliness, how she knew Michael was late because Charlotte had asked for extra tuition. She wanted to tell him she often felt as though she was frozen behind a layer of ice, trying to get out, trying to reach out to him, and her father's disappointment and her grandmother's distaste...

At that moment, Clive threw the glass against the wall and the ice around her seemed to shatter, crack loudly in the still air.

'Well?' He was shouting now, but she knew he was shouting in fear, in fear of the instability he could see opening up within her and around her. She wanted to reassure him, to take him back to the safety of their bed.

'Are you still in love with him?'

'Clive...'

He stroked Sebastian absent-mindedly and went to lay on the lounge. The jet lag engulfed him.

The phone rang a few hours later; it was Gustav, he sounded agitated, almost distressed. Alonso had died, and now Walter was using his increased vote to make changes – changes which would, Gustav feared, damage the bank irreparably.

Gustav had called Clive to ask him to talk to this Palmer fellow and try and get the ad campaign back on track... Gustav needed, somehow, to show the Board that he was still, very much, the head of Feldmann's. Could Clive come to Grenoble?

Clive showered, packed his bag and headed for the airport. He couldn't bear to stay in the house any longer. The first flight went at 8.40.

Drinking coffee in the Club Class lounge, his mobile vibrated in his pocket. He checked the number – 'unknown'. Nic had called six times – she didn't leave a message. He listened to his message.

'Oh – hello? Monsieur Alwynn? This is Mme. Géroux – the – uh – the housekeeper for Monsieur Feldmann – he – uh – he is very ill – he – he has asked that you join us. Do you think you might call me?' Clive stared at the phone, ignoring the prompt to delete the message.

CHAPTER 23

Virginia wandered about the apartment, picking up Ben's toys and clearing glasses and plates from the table.

The meal with Clive had been difficult – not only because Jack refused to join them, but because, after Ben had gone to bed and Clive and her were left alone, there was nothing to say that wasn't angry or loaded or part of the dangerous territory she thought she'd left behind when she moved to New York.

He'd looked tired, but that was probably the jet lag. Really, it seemed as if he hadn't aged at all. He must be happy in his work, or maybe Nicole made him happy? She shuddered slightly. She had tried *so* hard.

'Dammit' she shouted, banging down the dustbin lid. No matter how hard she tried, she could not suppress the images of Clive and Nicole that sprang into her mind, without warning, but with a sickening impact. Not every day any more – sometimes she even went for a week without thinking of them. Her doctor saw this as a sign of great improvement.

She'd never met Nicole. Clive had emailed out of the blue one day in March, not long after they'd divorced, to say he was getting married. No invitation, no offer of the boys attending. A mutual friend sent a picture later.

Nicole was nothing like Virginia. Smiling serenely, she was lean and tall. There was something 'still' about her, especially compared to Clive's happiness – he looked as if he might burst out of the picture on the sheer force of his joy. She looked untroubled – how had Virginia described her to her mother? –

'A woman with no baggage,' she'd said, trying to keep the bitter note from her voice.

Over dinner she'd asked Clive about the house, the dog and the cat. 'Oh, fine,' he'd said. 'Bella's as crazy as ever! She's really taken to Nic…'

'Good.'

'Ginnie – about Jack – '

'Oh, don't worry. It's just a shock to see you.'

'He mentioned Sebastian. Maybe he should come over and visit soon? I know Nic would…'

'Don't you *dare*, ' she said darkly and quietly. 'Don't you *dare* to even think about sitting in *our* house, with *our* children, and *our* pets, with your new wife. That will never happen.'

Clive was clearly shocked. 'Ginnie – they're my sons.'

'And did you care about that when we left? No. You did nothing. You let us walk away. And that was that. You had your chance and you chose not to take it.'

Clive raised his voice. 'They are my sons.'

She smiled bitterly. 'Did you feel so strongly when you decided to marry again? Do you imagine I *like* being alone, Clive? I will not put the boys through further disintegration of our family. The papers are signed. I'm afraid you and your wife will have to create your own lives. You're not having mine.'

'It's not that cut and dried, Ginnie. *Their* family has changed. The boys will adapt. The papers cite 'reasonable' access. Don't make me fight you on this.'

She laughed sarcastically. 'You've never fought for anything, Clive. You just took what came to you and moved on when it didn't work.'

'Jesus Christ, Ginnie! Where is all this coming from. *You* left *me*, for God's sake!'

'Oh, right. Saint Clive the Martyr. Listen,' she was close to tears of rage now. 'You left me a long time before I got in that cab. Oh, sure, you came home every night. But you were never *there*. Even before Ben was born. Maybe before Jack. I don't know. I try not to think about it anymore.'

Now it was late. After 1am. And Clive had left with the promise she'd be hearing from his lawyer. She could see Jack's reading lamp was still on. She took a deep breath, tried to stop shaking, and went to kiss her son goodnight.

CHAPTER 24

Robert Jeffreys looked out across the City of London. The
midday sun was already fading into an early grey dusk,
bouncing off the endless patchwork of reflective glass; slowly,
the interior lights outglowed the exterior. He watched the
thousands of workers struggling at their terminals. It was like
a beehive; yes, that's it, he thought. The struggle, the
constant building.

He'd cancelled his later appointments and asked Natalie to get
his driver around the front as quickly as possible. He was
tired. Natalie buzzed him and he took the elevator to the
ground floor.

His driver nodded and opened the door to the Mercedes.
There was no need for questions as to his destination; Natalie
would have sorted the details. Home. He was going home.

Polly would be waiting. Natalie had called her to say he was
on his way. She'd ask Mrs T to leave early – Polly knew how
much he hated her fussing about.

He watched the evening descend as the car powered up the
M40. He fidgeted with his Blackberry, flicked through a file or
two, but, in the end, sighed and fell back into the soft leather
seat. He was tired. The Doctors had said that he would feel
'fatigued', suffer from loss of concentration and memory loss.
He couldn't remember the other symptoms.

As the car pulled up into the Chiltern Hills, he half-smiled out
at the Beech trees jumping out into the headlights around
every corner. He and Polly had bought the house almost 20
years ago – just after the kids had gone to Uni. Justin did law

at Cambridge, Jocelyn did Economics at Oxford. Not that either of them had done anything with the degrees. The car pulled into the long gravel drive. The front light was on, and Mrs T's car gone. Polly, he smiled. Lovely Polly. What would he have done without her?

She met him at the front door.

'What's happening? Are you alright?' she took his coat.

'I'm fine. I needed to be home. Here.' He looked at her and kissed her passionately.

'Good. How do you feel?'

'Oh,' he waved a dismissive hand. 'Dizzy. Forced myself to eat a sandwich – but I'm not hungry Poll.' He saw the fear in her eyes.

'Well you'd bloody better be! Mrs T is sorely pissed that she had to rush the food tonight. And then, to boot, she had to fuck off.'

He laughed loudly. 'Right! Then let's eat! But, please. I need a drink.'

'Sure, but not too much. Why don't you go change and we'll have a jacuzzi?'

He smiled, stroked her hair, and kissed her forehead. Polly was not a beautiful woman, he thought, as he climbed the stairs to their bedroom. Not in the conventional sense. Not like his first wife had been. Mandy was a model when he met her; she was tall and willowy and blonde in a Marianne

Faithfull sort of way. He was an accountant for one of London's new record companies; record companies hoping to do what the big record companies had done for bands like the Beatles and the Stones.

Mandy loved the parties, and he saw that his colleagues were shocked that such a studious, numbers-focused weirdo could get her. But when the company went bust, no one cared about Robert and his wispy wife. And when Mandy found herself pregnant, the photographers stopped calling. That's when it all began to unravel.

Robert was happy to retire from the party lifestyle. He smiled to think of time with Mandy and the new baby. Jocelyn was a happy baby – bonnie? Wasn't that what the old nurses had called her? Imagine such a skinny mother producing this strong creature. Justin followed soon after – more like his mother: pale, willowy. They moved to a smaller house – just for a while, until Robert could sign that special band that would turn their luck around. The phone rang less and less, fewer and fewer friends came for dinner, and Mandy grew more and more dependent on the pills her 'agent' brought round, along with his promises of Vogue covers and this or that premier. Mixed with alcohol, the pills left her numb and mute, and she grew grey and bloated. Robert loved his children, and he worked hard to give them some sort of stability; family holidays, even if it was only the English seaside. He was home before they got back from school to cook, and to clean up Mandy who was often to be found unconscious in a pool of her own vomit.

Polly called from downstairs. 'Honey? Come on. The jacuzzi's pumpin'!'

'Here I am!' he called.

They lay back in the bubbling water, sipping Champagne.

Polly smiled. 'I'm sure the doctor would be happy to see you taking it easy.'

He laughed quietly. 'Yeah, sure. The champagne would really please him.'

'Who cares,' she laughed. 'Oh yes, Justin called today.'

'Oh – what did he want?'

'He wanted to see how you were...'

'And?'

'And he needs money...'

'Shit.' Robert sat forward and splashed water into face. 'What for this time?'

'He didn't say. I guess he'll tell you on Sunday.'

'Sunday?'

She reached across the pool and touched his cheek. 'It's your birthday, my love. Justin will be here, and Jocelyn and the kids. It's your 65th. You were born in Sydenham in 19 –'

'Alright!' he stepped out of the water. 'I'm not hungry...' he waved away her protests. 'Let's watch TV. I need to hold you...'

Robert climbed the stairs to the den and half-heartedly punched the buttons of the remote control. He was tired. Was it just the illness? Or was it the 'backlash', that creature that followed him like a dark shadow? He shook off the chill. The shadow first appeared at the same time that Mandy had died; after that he'd signed his first band – the first of many. Within weeks, Jocelyn and Justin were at boarding school. Then the storm, then Polly - the calm.

The phone rang, and went immediately to ansaphone.

'Hello. It's Jason Swift. I wonder if you'd give me a call...' and the caller rang off.

Polly came in carrying a tray of sandwiches.

'Who was that?' Robert asked. 'Swift, was it?'

'Oh, I don't know. Probably someone selling us something. Come here. You've got to eat.' And she tousled his hair gently.

CHAPTER 25

Nicole lay on the bed, riding out her hangover – a rising panic in her chest, and her muscles constricting around her throat.

She knew all she had to do was look at the bedroom in a different way – there – there was the picture of Clive and her, there were the lamps they chose together – they were always too bright. There, the glass of water Clive kept by his side of the bed; Sebastian curled in eiderdown.

The last light of the day hammered through the curtains. She plunged again into that chest-constraining panic.

Where was Clive?

So, it had happened – he'd left her. She always knew he would. She stumbled to the bathroom, and forced herself to look at her reflection in the mirror. She thought she might be beautiful, even in this distress. Perhaps because of it? She saw the classic lines, the classic brunette, the nose her father had, once or twice, kissed as he told her stories of her mother – but only when he'd been drinking.

She needed coffee, but doubted she could keep the paracetamol down. She thought of Michael, and their unborn baby. 'Stop it!' she shouted to herself.

Bella was standing at the back door, miming panic through the double-glazing. 'Come in!' she cried, and the dog's muddy feet left a trail across the white kitchen floor. She went through to the lounge and snuggled into the corner seat. Bella fell on top of her, while Sebastian criss-crossed the floor by her feet, his tail an indifferent question mark.

Cyn knocked at the door, excitedly. 'Oh my God! You poor darling,' she cried as she hugged Nicole. 'You look crap!' Nicole half-smiled, comparing her M&S blue-checked pyjamas to Cyn's immaculate black trousers, black cashmere sweater and black beret set beautifully on her round head.

'Sit down,' she called from the kitchen. 'You need some food and a hair of the dog, honey.'

'Uggghhh! No,' protested Nicole. 'I feel like shit.'

'Exactly *why* you need a hair of the dog. Do you have any eggs?'

'I'm not hungry, really Cyn...'

'No! It's a hangover cure: tomato juice, vodka, egg....'

'I'm not eating a raw egg in this country, Cyn. Didn't you hear about a little problem called Salmonella a while back?'

'No, but it's not a problem,' she said, reappearing from the kitchen. 'You don't have any eggs. Nor do you have Tabasco. Or lemons. Here, get this into you and tell me everything. Where is he? What the hell happened?' She unwrapped the chips and sausages she'd picked up at the local kebab shop.

Nicole shook her head, braced herself for a shot of this abridged Bloody Mary. She told Cyn about the whole horrible evening.

'Jesus. Well it sounds to me like he's being a baby!' Cyn declared, waving a sausage at Nicole. 'Honestly. It's not as though he didn't *know* about Michael. I think I told him before you did... sorry,' she smiled at Nicole's annoyance.

'It's not Michael *per se*,' she sighed. 'It's the whole termination thing.'

'Oh God, don't tell me he's anti-choice?'

'No, no. It's the fact that I didn't tell him about the abortion….'

'Oh,' Cyn inhaled heavily on her cigarette. 'And why *was* that exactly?'

'I don't know… it just seemed to … I don't know. There just seemed to be so much darkness surrounding that time… I didn't want to bring that in to Clive's world.'

'Don't you think he can handle it?'

Nicole fidgeted with the tassel of the cushion. 'Of course he can handle it! He's been through his own drama with the divorce for God's sake...'

'Well, from what I remember, from what Giles has told me, he didn't really handle it at all. Not in the way you and I might. He ran away from it.'

'Bullshit. Virginia ran away from it. She took the boys and moved to the States.'

'Yeah, and Clive let her.'

'Jesus, Cyn. I'm not really in the mood for this today.' She started to cry.

'I'm sorry, Hon. Come here, let me top up this drink. All I'm saying is that maybe on some level you didn't think Clive could handle it. Maybe you can't handle it? I'm assuming this is not about Michael? Seeing him the other night...'

'No. Anything I felt for him is dead and gone. I mean, I can see why I fell for him... but, it's more... it's more the *betrayal*, I think.'

'But you can't be sure he cheated on you...'

'No. But even if he didn't – there's some sort of emotional betrayal. He pulled away from me... I felt...'

Cyn exhaled. ' Nic, you never loved Michael. Maybe that's why he pulled away?'

Nicole looked confused, but Cyn continued on.

'It's a role you're playing here, honey. Abandoned. As abandoned as the little girl who's father sent her to live with her Grandmother.'

Nicole nodded through her sobs.

'It doesn't take a genius to figure this out girlfriend,' sighed Cyn, holding Nicole in her arms tightly. 'Your mother abandoned you, your father abandoned you, Michael abandoned you... then you abandoned your baby...'

Nicole's body convulsed in sobs as she buried her head deeper into the cushion.

'Jesus,' Cyn sighed. 'There's more abandonment here than Battersea Dogs' Home!'

Nicole laughed despite herself. 'Yeah, it's a freaking soap-opera. But what am I gonna do Cyn?'

'You're gonna get some sleep, wake up and sort this shit out. Give him a day or two to calm down and then track him down – his office will know where he is. Don't worry – it's gonna be fine once you two actually talk to each other. And once you both get the balls to trust each other...'

Nicole fell into a deep sleep. When she woke, it was dark, the side lamps on and the animals were sleeping contentedly on the floor. Cyn must have fed them before she left, she thought.

The ansaphone light flashed furiously; she reached over and hit play. It was Clive.

'Oh, thank God!' she thought.

'Nic,' he said. 'Listen. I'm in Grenoble. This Feldmann's thing is mad. Can't get the mobile reception up here. I think I need a couple of days to... sort things out. Everything just seems so...Anyway. I'll call you in a couple of days. Bye.'

The end-of-message beep sounded more like a long, sad groan. Nicole stared at the machine.

CHAPTER 26

Jason Swift liked jazz. Sax. Rainy night, big city, neon signs jazz. His office was a tiny room, up a few flights of stairs, on Tottenham Court Road. Nights like tonight, he could look out at the HMV sign across the way and really believe he was in Chicago... or New York.

It was after 1am, and he'd decided to sleep in the office again. He pressed play on the CD and Miles Davis' Sketches of Spain floated up on a cloud of cigarette smoke. He poured himself a whiskey.

He slept in the office more and more often – since his wife had had the baby, the flat in Finchley had become alien; a place of soft pink smells, white fluffy cotton and, more often than not, tears. Not just the newborn's crying, but his wife's, too.

He'd installed a sofa bed in the office last month, happy to think he'd have somewhere to crash after one of his all-night surveillance jobs. Not that he'd *had* an office before this September gone.

This new account had been manna from heaven... lump sum up front, and the client had been so paranoid about security, they'd added enough to allow Jay to rent this tiny office – short term, but now, as he leafed through his notes, he knew he'd be able to pay for an extension to the lease. Manna. From. Heaven. He blew another smoke ring into the air. And the case was a piece of piss: all he had to do was follow this guy and log his days. Where he went, who he saw. He was not required to make any judgements – not like he did on his normal cases. 'Yes, Mrs Jones, I do believe, based on the fact your husband had his hands down the woman's blouse even before they entered the reception of the cheap hotel, that, yes, your husband is a lousy, cheating scumbag. That'll be £250 thank you.'

No. This case was much easier money.

He followed the guy to his office early most mornings, hung around the pub across the road for the long day, then followed him home to Highgate. The guy led a pretty dull life, in Jay's opinion. Too much work, and certainly not enough time with that wife of his. She was older, sure, but a hot old. Sort of like Michelle Pfeiffer. And then there was his late night visit to the accountant broad's cottage.

Over the last months he'd gotten to know his target quite well, he thought. He'd gone the standard route – raid the bins, chat to the receptionist in the office – glorious tits, loose mouth. And sitting in the pub, nursing a long pint, reaped pages of reports for his client. It seemed that every smart-ass media type who spent their lunch hour over a pint mentioned Clive Alwynn. Seemed he was a bit of a big-shot round the office.

Well, from what Jay Swift could see he was a puffed up nothing. Sure, he was tall, sort of handsome, but something about him disturbed Swift. It was his... cockiness. Yes, that was it. These advertising types, they made a clever phrase, a clever line, and they earned the mega-bucks. It was guys like Jay, guys who worked quietly and meticulously in the shadows who deserved more; more than these cocks. He stubbed out his cigarette and emailed his client.

'Subject travelled today to Grenoble again today. Happy to follow. Please advise.'

CHAPTER 27

Palmer slid into James' office, closing the door behind him.

'James, this Feldmann's account is really going happen, isn't it?' And he clapped his hands together greedily.

James nodded confidently. 'Yes. I think they really get the new pitch, Alex. Well done. What the fuck was wrong with Alwynn? How could he have been so wrong on the direction? Thank God you were here.'

Palmer sighed. 'I don't know, James. I have tried with Clive… but he's terribly defensive. Doesn't make for a good 'team player', you know. My creatives have been having a terrible time of it. They find him hard to read… don't understand what it is he's trying to do.'

James looked concerned. 'That's not good. I want you to keep an eye on this…'

Palmer wanted more than this half-arsed acknowledgement that the account was his – at least in theory. He went in for the kill.

'Oh sure, James. You know I will. There's too much riding on this. But I should tell you – oh, I don't know. Maybe it's nothing…'

'What? Out with it Palmer – as you said, there's too much riding on this!'

Palmer looked resigned. 'OK. A friend of mine works in New York – Stansons.'

'The publishers?'

'Yes. Well it seems they're branching out – there's talk of an advertising arm.'

'Yes, yes….'

'Well,' Palmer raised his eyebrows a little, and dropped his voice to a near whisper. 'Alwynn's ex-wife works for them, and…'

'Yes – she took his boys with her didn't she? Nasty business.'

'Yes. Well, my friend in Stansons says they're looking at Clive to head up the new arm.'

'What!' James exploded. 'Ungrateful bastard! He's been busting my balls for the last three months to head up a fucking account and now he's jumping ship?'

'Yes – it certainly looks like it, James. I believe he interviewed yesterday.'

James was livid. 'OK Palmer, that's it. Effective now – you take Feldmann's. I want Alwynn off it.'

He strode from the room, ranting to himself, and cursing his mobile as it rang.

Palmer smiled and checked his watch. It was only mid-morning, but he'd had a long day, and decided it was long past lunchtime.

******

Rachel stirred the butter into the mashed potatoes. Ben sat on a stool, concentrating on the letter he was writing. Mr Porkie sat defiantly on the edge of the breakfast bar; Rachel had long given up on moving him. They'd reached an agreement: Mr Porkie perched at the edge never advancing, and Rachel ignored him. Had Virginia been home, she'd have thrashed him with the dishcloth.

'Rachel?' said Ben. 'How do you say "visit with us" in English?'

She rinsed the fork under the tap. 'Visit with us? Well, you say "Visit with us", I guess. Why?'

'I'm writing to daddy – I said: "Mr Porkie and I would like you to come visit with us again. Jack does not want you to come, but mommy says I can follow my own path ...'

'Ben,' Rachel dried her hands on the towel. 'Supper time.'

'But I need to ...'

'Ben! Come on. Mommy will be home soon. We need you fed and ready for bed. Jack! Come on!'

'OK!' Jack called. He logged off the computer. He'd logged into Clive's company's site. His dad was very important. Not the boss, but very important. He knew by the photo on the site that his dad was very happy in his job. He knew his dad was very happy in his new life, with a lady called Nic. His new life without Jack. His new life without Ben. Without mommy. Poor mommy.

'Damn cat!', he shouted. Mr Porkie looked nonplussed and fluffed out his fur to stand his ground. 'Ben, for god's sake! I'm telling mommy. You shouldn't let Mr Porkie up here!'

'Sebastian always sat at the end of the table,' said Ben defensively. He signed off his letter: 'Maybe if you can't come to our place, I can visit with you in England.'

He sealed the letter and put it on the hall table, like he always did. He wanted to believe that this time his dad would answer, but he was already losing faith as he climbed back onto his stool and sunk his spoon into the mashed potato.

Jack was telling Rachel about today's swimming competition, as she washed the pots and pans.

Virginia's key turned in the front door. As she took off her coat and pushed her shopping bags to one side, she held the boys. 'Hey, my boys!' They clung to her and Mr Porkie slunk off to his basket in the lounge.

Rachel smiled, said goodnight to them all. She took her coat from the hall cupboard and picked up Ben's letter from the table, slipping it discreetly into her pocket. She headed out into the night, touching the envelope in her pocket: this one *would* reach Ben's dad, she decided.

CHAPTER 28

Polly Jeffreys watched her husband from the kitchen window. He was wandering about the wintery garden, smoking a small cigar – against his doctor's advice – and seemed to be mumbling to himself.

They'd enjoyed a slow start to his 65th birthday – champagne and croissants in bed, and a long session of love-making. Robert's drug regime made it difficult for him, but he relished the pleasure his hands and mouth could give his wife. And he wanted to give her so much before he died.

She turned away and grabbed the oven glove. The hors-d'oeuvres were nearly done; perfect. Justin and Jocelyn were due any minute. She knew Justin would be late, and she knew he'd be high on cocaine.

The doorbell rang and Jocelyn and her children came tumbling in. 'Hey Polly! Jamie, bring the baby's bottles, too, honey. Kids? Say hello to Grandma Polly!'

Three children under the age of 10 rushed forward with a cheer, and Polly scooped them up greedily, breathing them in. 'Hello, little ones!' Jocelyn's husband, Jamie, struggled in, loaded up with bags and toys and assorted jackets and cardigans. 'Hi Polly!' he called cheerily. Jocelyn was already in the kitchen, pulling the hors-d'oeuvres from the oven. 'These look perfect, Poll.'

Polly bit her tongue; Jocelyn had always had a problem with boundaries. All through her teens Polly had asked her to stay out of the kitchen when she was cooking, but Jocelyn had seemed indifferent to anyone else's needs or wishes. Of course, she was only trying to be 'helpful', but it still made Polly grind her teeth. 'Yes, thanks... have you said hello to your father?' Jocelyn rolled her eyes, just as she had through most of her teen years. 'No – where is he? Hiding in the garden, I suppose? You *know* he hates parties, Poll.'

Polly ignored the barb and slammed the oven door shut, just as Justin came bounding into the room.

'Hey Poll! Jocie! God the traffic was bad, I don't know if it's the congestion charge or what, but I swear more people are driving nowadays...'

'Hello Justin,' said Polly. 'Isn't the congestion charge designed to discourage drivers?'

'Aha!' he shouted. 'That's what you're supposed to think, Poll. It's that bloody mayor! Bloody lefties – they learned their mind control tricks from the Russians, you know! Hey! Jamie! Where are my nephews? And my niece?' And he was gone.

'Jesus,' said Polly under her breath. He's completely stoned. She watched Jocelyn stroking her father's hair and patting his round belly. It made her angry – not jealous, just angry. She was, according to Robert, 'her mother's daughter'. Despite having been a chubby baby, she was a handsome woman, curvy, yet almost slender, even after three children. But she was an incredibly selfish individual.

Polly recalled her as a teenager, always wanting, demanding, and whining. *Entitled.* That's what Polly had called her. Robert had never been able to say no to her. Things got out of control when Mandy died. Jocelyn was 13 and Justin 12, so they came to live with Robert and Polly. It became too easy to blame all of their appalling behaviour on grief, and, eventually, Polly gave up, relieved when they returned to their boarding schools.

She looked out of the window and watched Justin flinging one of his nephews into the air, dangerously high, as Jamie stood by nervously, looking from Justin to Jocelyn, undecided as to who might help the situation. Polly slammed the oven door shut.

'Robert!' she bellowed. 'Can you come in and give me a hand?' Jocelyn smirked in an exaggerated fashion as Robert disentangled himself from her hugs and walked through the garden, completely ignoring the little boy's cries for help as his uncle threw him into the air once again.

'Yes, love. Are you alright in here?' Robert looked about, as helpless as ever in the kitchen.

Polly smiled. 'Fine. I thought you'd like to get everyone a drink?'

'Oh, yes, of course… God, Polly, those hors-d'oeuvres look fantastic… even if that's all there was it would be enough.'

She smiled. 'Well there's a roast to follow, so don't overdo it. How's Jocelyn?' and she pretended to busy herself, brushing the potatoes with oil.

'Oh, you know…' he pulled the cork from the Chardonnay. 'They're broke.' The cork popped out. 'Again.'

'Oh, no. I thought Jamie was doing some consultancy work?'

'Well, he was, but it seems he couldn't cut it. I really don't know what Jocelyn sees in him, Polly.'

She looked out to the garden. Jocelyn had caught her son and was now firmly rebuking Jamie for his total inability to do even the smallest thing for his children. All she'd wanted was to spend a little time with her father, but could she leave him in charge of the children, no. Jamie seemed to shrink by another inch.

'Oh, I don't know, Robert. It might be a good idea for Jocelyn to go back to work. I mean, they have the nanny now...'

'No, they fired her. She reckons she was stealing.' He saw Polly roll her eyes. 'I know, darling. I know. But, hey? She doesn't know it, but she'll inherit a substantial sum within the next six months.'

'Shut up!' Polly surprised herself with the sharpness of her voice. 'Please Robert. Let's not talk like that – not today. Not on your birthday?'

'I'm sorry darling,' and he held her tightly. 'Don't worry. I've told her she can have 5k for the minute, but that's it. I'm sure she'll wait until I have another drink and start in on me again.'

'Are you still sure that you won't leave Justin anything?'

Robert sighed. 'Have you seen him yet? Completely fucked. I've told him he won't get another loan out of me until I see he's cleaned up his act. Anything I give him now will just go up his nose. And that won't change once I'm gone... the lawyers will hold the money in Trust. His uncle Damian will decide when – if – he ever gets it.'

'Hmmmm. I know why you're doing it, but I think he'll just read it as you being a bastard.'

'Sure he will,' and he laughed. 'But I don't care. Look Polly, darling. I love those kids dearly, but I know what they are. I know their faults. And god knows I'm responsible for most of those of those faults.'

She touched his face gently. 'OK. Now go and call them into the lounge for drinks – I've put some soft drinks in the games room for the kids.'

As he wandered back to the garden, she was overwhelmed with sadness that he would indeed soon be gone. But as she carried the tray into the lounge, she was more resolved than ever that she'd make sure that, at the time of his passing, he was happy. And complete. She'd close the circle; shine a light and wipe away the shadow that followed him.

CHAPTER 29

Nicole knocked at Professor Dower's office door.

'Come in, Nicole. Sit down. How are things?'

Shannon Dower was mid-fifties, with long, lustrous hair and a body committed to macrobiotics and extreme exercise. Being Head of the Literature Department meant she couldn't work out at the gym as often as she would have liked; so she'd taken up running and now averaged a ten-mile run every morning, and something close to a half-marathon every weekend. The lack of excess fat made her look a little older than she was, but, Nicole thought, the visible strength and tautness of her muscles was actually quite sexy.

Nicole smiled. 'Oh, fine.'

'Well your classes seem to be going well – good results on last semester's papers and no student harassment claims...'

They laughed.

'Well,' said Nicole. 'I wondered if I could ask for a little time off?'

'Sure – your classes are off on revision next week...'

'Yes, but I wondered if I could also have the week after that? I know I promised you the book wouldn't interfere with my duties here, but I have a wonderful lead from a museum up in Derbyshire, and . . .'

'Nicole! Please... you have been nothing less than generous in the amount of time you've given us, and we've really appreciated it. I sometimes feel a little guilty that we haven't supported your research more! But you know what it's like ... funding cuts, less staff...'

'Oh, Shannon, please! You've been wonderful. I just need this week.'

'Absolutely. Nicole, I hope you don't mind me asking, but ... is everything alright? At home? Clive?'

Nicole looked defiant at her mothering tone, but fell back into her chair, realising that the dark shadows under her eyes and the fact that she hadn't washed her hair this morning was a dead-giveaway of domestic dysfunction.

'No, everything's rather awful at the moment...' she stammered.

'Right,' said Shannon. 'That's decided then. Take the extra week... take two extra weeks. We can write you off with a flu... students will love an extra week of study leave. After that, I can probably get one of the other Lecturers to take the next week...'

'Thank you, Shannon,' Nicole smiled.

'Not a problem. Just do what you need to do and then come back to us.'

So, that was that. The bus groaned its way back to Highgate. Nicole had hardly enough strength to walk up the drive.

Bella danced in the window, and she felt a strange pang of guilt to be leaving her and Sebastian to the visiting service. Oh, she liked the woman enough and knew that she could be relied on, but she knew that this would be how it felt when she *really* left. When she left this house. When she left Clive. Her husband.

She checked the ansaphone. No messages. She called the trainline and booked a first-class ticket to Derbyshire. She packed her suitcase – enough clothes for three weeks. She called the cab company and booked a cab to Euston for noon. She showered and fell into a deep sleep.

The next morning, the alarm buzzed. She jumped up and grabbed at the phone.

'Oh God.'

She held Bella's huge head in her hands, stroked Sebastian's tail as it snaked around her calf, and hurried out to the cab.

She was glad she'd chosen first class; she had a table and no one sitting near her. She opened up her laptop and reviewed William Hartnett's last email. The Curator of the small museum in Elizabeth's hometown had sent her an excited email last week. It seemed that the great granddaughter of Mrs Ann Roswell – the Vicar's wife responsible for the parish newsletter which had announced Elizabeth's departure for the United States, had passed away, leaving all of her books, journals and history of the village to the local museum.

William Hartnett sounded very excited in his email – he had uncovered something rather unexpected, and hoped that Nicole would be able to come up and discuss. He also wondered if, in exchange, she might not be willing to present her current research at the Stanton by Bridge Historical Society meeting on Thursday night?

Nicole sighed and slammed the laptop shut. The steward refilled her glass, and she looked out across the gently rolling green of Derbyshire. Snapshots of her Grandmother's home came to her... the long, manicured lawns that stretched down to the apple orchard, and then further to the wild hills, the dales to where she'd escaped so many afternoons.

She wondered about Clive. Why had he told her he needed space? Surely he could not believe that she was still in love with Michael Forester? Maybe Clive had found someone else? No; she knew he was not the type to play around, despite the opportunities he had. Tall, good looking, charming... Nicole had watched him at parties or in restaurants, and watched the effect he had on the women around him. But she knew he would not cheat on her. She fought back the tears. 'Damn him,' she thought. 'Is this what happened to Virginia? He just turned tail and ran as soon as it got complicated?' She remembered what Cyn had said...

Before she knew it, the train had arrived at Derby. William had promised he'd greet her on the platform, and she scanned the small crowd for an old, professorial looking gentleman. Someone tapped her on the shoulder. 'Dr Alwynn?'

She turned to face a young, red-haired, man – no more than 30 years old. 'Dr Alwynn? William Hartnett. It's such a pleasure to meet you.' He shook her hand wildly and then grabbed her bag and hurried out the exit to the car park. 'We're parked just over here...

He put her bag into the boot of the old Volvo, and they set off.

'How was your trip? I hope the train food was of the normal standard because we've arranged lunch for you …'

'Mr Hartnett. William… If it's all the same with you, I really would prefer to go straight to my hotel. It's been a long week, I …'

'Oh.' He blushed again. 'I imagined, you being a researcher… um, the trustees provide me with a large house… just next door to the museum. I assumed you'd stay …'

'What?' Nicole shook her head uncomprehendingly. 'Look, Mr Hartnett… I don't need your charity. I'm actually a *Lecturer* at the University of London. Perhaps the local pub has a room?'

William Hartnett swallowed his panic, and pretended to concentrate on driving. 'The *local* pub is about 20 miles away from the village – they all closed down. Stanford's more of a hamlet than a town. The Post Office went years ago.'

'Jesus,' said Nicole, sighing into her hands.

'Oh, please!' William imagined what it was to look reassuring. 'Just let's go back to lunch at my place – the house – and if you want to stay in the pub, I'll drive you there straight after. I wouldn't be so insistent, it's just that Mrs Jacobs, the lady who cleans the house, made a terrible fuss about you staying – it meant she had to prepare a room, the linen and her husband's off work with his back, so she's had to tend to the cows, and I just pissed her off big time by asking if she'd mind putting together a few things for lunch.'

Nicole looked at him incredulously. 'Is this your normal welcome speech for visiting academics?'

'Oh no, no not at all,' he shook his head rapidly. 'No. Normally the Trustees give us a few extra pounds so we can stretch to a little wine. But that's when the visitor's really important. Usually a Bronte connection. So if you could just come to lunch and tell Mrs J how wonderful it was... you'd be making my life so much easier. And besides, I so want to talk you through the Parnell materials I've discovered.'

Nicole laughed, despite herself. 'OK, William... and, please, call me Nicole.'

They pulled up outside a small greystone cottage on a narrow main street. Today was market day and so the traffic congestion was as bad as London's. William carried her bag to the door and searched for his keys. Once inside, the noise from the street fell away, thanks to the double glazing, and he led Nicole down a short hall to the kitchen.

'Mrs J?' William called. 'Mrs J?'

Nicole nodded to the note on the table. 'I think Mrs J has left the building...'

'Ahhh,' said William, realising how dodgy the situation looked. 'She did say she'd be here... if you like I can drive you to the pub...'

Nicole laughed and sighed. 'No, no, no. I'm too tired to bother. If you could show me to my room, I can get settled in and maybe we can talk shop over lunch?'

William looked relieved. 'Yes, oh yes. Good!'

He led the way up a narrow, dark staircase to a small, simply decorated room with a large single bed in the centre, and a bedside table with a lamp.

'Oh, it's lovely!' said Nicole, delighted with the pale blue walls, and the hand-made quilt. 'Thanks William. And look, I'm sorry I was so rude in the car. It's been a rough week...'

'Sure. Come down when you're ready. I've got so much to tell you about Elizabeth! Oh, the bathroom's along the hall to your left.'

She unpacked, washed her face and tied her hair back again. Downstairs, William had laid out Mrs J's lunch – a meagre and cold selection of ham, pickles, cheese and bread.

'Well,' she smiled at his embarrassment. 'I'm clearly not Bronte enough!' They laughed and he held up a bottle of Cabernet Sauvignon. 'Clearly, but it's a virtual banquet with a glass or two of this, Dr Alwynn!'

'So, tell me about Elizabeth,' she smiled as they built sandwiches.

'Oh no... she's your specialty Nicole! How did you find her?'

She put the small box on the table, and unwrapped the leather-bound notebook. 'The pages are so fragile,' she said.

'I've had all the pages scanned, but a computer file has nothing compared to the feel of this paper.'

'Wow,' he spoke quietly, reverentially. 'Yes. I know what you mean. You need to put acid-free paper between these pages, Nicole. And I wouldn't be transporting this around the country...'

'No, I normally don't I work from an A4 print-out of the scans. I just thought you'd like to see the real thing.'

'Oh, God, yes. It's absolutely gorgeous,' he sighed, running a finger down the leather cover. 'So what's the poetry like?'

'It's funny you said 'poetry',' she looked a little confused. 'What makes you think it's poems?'

William smiled. His pallid cheeks were flushed deep red, thanks to the wine and the central heating which had kicked in just as the day faded.

'Well, now it's my turn to impress *you*. And to show you why I wanted you to come all the way to Derbyshire...'

He rose, and hurried into the sitting room. 'It's probably best to come through here, Nicole.' He turned on the large lamp on the side table. 'Sit down,' he gestured to a little sofa in the corner, and sat on the floor near her feet. 'Look,' he smiled, anticipating her amazement. 'Look. Elizabeth's books...'

He unwrapped three neatly bound, leather books – identical to the one she held.

'Oh my god...' she put her hand to her mouth. 'Are you serious? How can you be sure? Is it really my Elizabeth....'

He laughed at her questions, and smiled as she gently turned the pages, recognition dawning on her expression. 'Oh my God....' she whispered, recognising the beautiful sloping letters and the definite long tails of each 'y', or 'j' – never a loop; just an uncompromising slash of a line cutting into the line below.

'What are these?' she looked up.

'Elizabeth's poetry – well, that's the first one. The other one's a diary...'

Nicole couldn't believe what she was hearing. 'A diary?'

'Yes, it starts at the time she comes back from the States...'

'Back? She came back?'

'Yes, it seems she spurned the husband her father had set up for her – I think it was her father's cousin's son....'

'God!' Nicole laughed. 'Look – can I ask you a favour? I know you want to tell me what you've read, but it's really important for me – for my book – that I read it directly from her diary. I need to hear Elizabeth's story from Elizabeth. Do you understand?'

'Indeed I do. That's why I took the liberty of copying both books. Here's a printout... but I should warn you – she doesn't give away a lot of details once she's back here. Poetry of course, but you get the sense she's not telling the whole story... well, at least I did.'

'Oh, William. You are so great!' And she leaned forward to grab his hand.

He blushed again. 'No, it's nothing really. Lord knows the Trustees would be overjoyed if we had our own 'Bronte' here in the village! Anyhow, I expect you'd like to go and read the books. I'll just clear up... I hope you sleep well. Tomorrow, I wondered if you'd like to go out to the Parnell's farm? The great-niece still lives there. She has a few good memories, stories to tell....'

Nicole smiled, hugged the printouts to her chest and thanked him again. She hadn't thought of Clive for the last three hours.

The next morning, she woke to the smell of fresh coffee and Radio 4. William was working on his laptop at the breakfast table.

'How did you sleep?' he smiled.

'Like a log,' she said, pouring herself a coffee. 'After I read the diary, of course... but I felt terribly guilty.'

'Guilty? Why?'

'Because I was a terrible guest last night, and did not have the courtesy to ask about my host!'

He laughed. 'Oh, there's nothing much to tell really,' he said, blushing. 'Born in Derry, went to Uni in London. History; First

Class Honours. Out to Colorado – Boulder. Did the Curatorship degree. Got the smallest museum possible, but it's paying back my student loan.'

'Impressive,' she smiled. 'I did a few years in the States. San Fran. What's your plan from here?'

'It'd be great to get another museum, but I'm afraid I'm crap at pleasing Trustees. It's an age-old thing: they want to preserve their past, their heritage, but they don't seem to get that it has to be interesting to an audience. They laugh at the Americans – the fake 'pioneer villages' and all, but, you know, these places get millions of visitors! Living history: that's what we need to show. Otherwise we're condemned to a poxy museum which can only afford to open two afternoons a week!'

'These will be the Trustees I'm meeting tomorrow night then,' she said, looking sceptical.

'Yes, yes. But lots more people are coming now that they know we have such an illustrious speaker!' He winked. 'However. Back to today. I told Mrs Previs we'd be out her way around 12? Is that ok? We'd need to leave in about half an hour.'

'Great. So, she's the great-niece… of Elizabeth?'

'Yes, Elizabeth's brother inherited the farm, of course. It's his daughter's daughter. She's very old now, 90s I think; very frail. She signed over a huge chest of stuff – books, notes, posters, records… all pertaining to the village. And Elizabeth's stuff of course.'

'Is she still 'with-it'? You know... '

'Sharp as a pin, I'm afraid.' He smiled at her confusion. 'She's quite a challenge...'

'Great. Well let me get my stuff and we'll be off, then.'

'Certainly. I see you brought a camera? Good.'

CHAPTER 30

William and Nicole wound their way up the undulating Dales, and at the peak, William stopped the car. 'Here. Bring your camera out...'

They stood at the crest of the hill; below them a vast patchwork of green fields rolled out to the far horizon. The sky was grey, but even so, it seemed to shine down on the boulder-studded slopes. 'God, it's beautiful.'

The Volvo wound its way up the long muddy track to Emily Previs's cottage. She sat in the front room, watching the skinny red-headed lad jump from the car and hurry around to open the passenger door, which was already opening. A tall-ish, slim woman stepped out of the car, pushing her sunglasses up onto her head and sweeping back her dark brown hair. So, this was the girlie looking for information about Elizabeth? Well, she wouldn't be getting much out of Emily Previs. Elizabeth might have lived an immoral existence, but she was family, and family had to stand together. She struggled to her feet and leaning heavily on her stick, she shuffled to the door.

'Ah, Mrs Previs! Hello!' shouted William. 'Do you remember I mentioned Dr Alwynn? The lady who is interested in your great Aunt?'

Nicole reached out her hand and began to say 'Lovely to meet you...' but was immediately interrupted by Emily.

'Of course I remember,' she responded tetchily. 'You only told me last week. And why are you shouting so much?'

'Oh,' William blushed. 'Right – you've got your hearing aid in today….'

'Of course I've got the blasted thing in. Where else would it be? Well come on then, there's tea in the kitchen, but it's probably gone cold now. I was expecting you ten minutes ago.'

'Yes, I'm sorry. I didn't realise the lower road had flooded – we took a detour.'

'Well sit down. Can you pour?' She looked to Nicole.

'Sure,' she smiled. 'Mrs Previs, I want to thank you for making time to see me. You've no idea how excited I am to be meeting Elizabeth's family.'

'Well, I'll be honest with you Miss; I don't understand what all the fuss is about. William here tells me you found an old journal in America? And then you travel all the way here to talk about her?'

'Yes, perhaps it does sound strange – but I fell in love with her poems, Mrs Previs. She was a really talented writer, I believe, and I want other people to know about her.'

'The family won't be happy with people knowing about her – that's a fact.'

Nicole looked to William in confusion. 'Why?'

Emily stirred a third teaspoon of sugar into her tea and pushed a plate of biscuits to the centre of the table. 'It was hard enough for my grandfather when she was alive, Miss.

They had to go to church every week knowing that everyone was whispering behind their hands, looking down on us.'

'Because Elizabeth didn't marry the man in America? Her father's cousin's son.'

'No, no, no! Because of the affair with Thomas!' Emily was irritable and looking forward to her afternoon nap. 'Elizabeth set up house with Thomas Ryland – the local teacher. The *married* local teacher.'

'Oh, I see,' Nicole nodded slowly.

'No, I'm not sure that you do. That would have been bad enough in itself, but they – she – she had his baby.'

'Oh, my – in those days….'

'And in these days, too! Most people round here have grown up knowing about the Parnell girl and her bastard.' She reached out for another biscuit. 'I got it at school: you know, the 'Parnell hussies' they used to call me and my cousins. I don't see what good it would be to stir it all up again – there's my children and their children to think about. I don't want them – or their neighbours - reading about it in a book.'

'I understand Mrs Previs, really I do but I think nowadays people will be much more sympathetic…'

'You won't find sympathy in this village – there's folks down there who would love to be reminded of Elizabeth's shame.'

Nicole smiled gently. 'But I'd be reminding them – telling them – about good things. The poetry – that would be something your family could be proud of.'

'Hmmm, well... I don't know why people would be interested in her words – but then I don't know anything about poetry and such.'

'Well, I promise you – her work is special. It will make you very proud to be a Parnell.'

'Never said I wasn't,' the old lady struggled to her feet. 'I'll ask my son what he thinks. He'll be over tonight, like every night. Now, if you don't mind, I'll ask you to leave. I have things to do...'

'Of course,' William stood up, shaking his head at Nicole to discourage any more questions. 'Do you mind then, Mrs Previs, if Nicole comes back tomorrow and looks around the farm a little? Just to get a feel for the place Elizabeth grew up?'

'No harm in that, I suppose. But you won't be writing your book until I talk to my son.'

William and Nicole were getting into the car, when the old lady shouted from the front door. 'And when you come, bring some cake from Little's!'

William laughed as they drove away. 'That's the village bakery. She probably doesn't get down there anymore.'

'Jesus,' sighed Nicole as they drove back into the village. 'Elizabeth Parnell had a child.'

'Yes, it's bloody amazing, isn't it? To a married man!'

'William, we've got to find out what happened to the kid. And to Thomas... God, I hope her son gives us the green light.'

'Oh, no problem if he won't – you've seen Emily. She's old and she's often miserable, but she likes a good natter. She won't be able to stop herself from telling you the whole story.'

'That sounds a little unethical!' Nicole raised her eyebrows incredulously.

William laughed. 'Well, if it's not Emily Previs we ask, we know that some of the old villagers will have a good enough idea of the story. It's in the public domain already, Nicole. The museum has the old school records, by the way. They came to us when the school closed in the 1960s. If Thomas was a teacher there, there may be something about him.'

'Great. I really want to know about his wife, too. I mean, I assume she knew this was going on? God, this is 'the secret' she keeps referring to. Thomas and her... it's a central theme of the poetry.'

'Yes, you're right – so the 'reaching out', the 'take my hand' – maybe that's the child she's talking to? Not her lover?'

'I don't know... but I'm going to have to look at the poems again – knowing what we know.'

'Or what we don't know,' he smiled.

'Yet,' she said firmly.

Back at the house, she went to her room and checked her phone, but there was no reception. What did it matter anyway? She knew Clive well enough to know that he wouldn't call her.

William stood in the doorway, and noticed her disappointment as she stared at the phone. 'Sorry – I ... um... I wondered. The Trustees' meeting doesn't start until 8pm. Do you fancy dinner at the pub first – it's a bit of a drive, but worth it.'

'Sure,' she smiled. 'That would be good.'

'Are you expecting a call?' he asked gently, nodding to the phone.

'Um... no... well, yes, I was hoping the woman looking after our dog and cat would have called. Just to tell me all is ok.'

'Oh, well use the landline in the kitchen. It's lousy for mobiles up here. Is it ok if we leave in about 20 minutes?'

Once he'd gone, she fell back on the bed and closed her eyes. Bella. Sebastian. Her eyes filled with tears. Clive. She sighed. She had to change and get her notes together for tonight's meeting. Hopefully it wouldn't take long, and she could come back here and hide away for a few hours. She was more interested in visiting Emily Previs tomorrow. Poor Elizabeth, she sighed. Nicole didn't know the full story, yet, but this evening she felt all the pain and the yearning of Elizabeth's poems.

CHAPTER 31

Jay Swift ordered another coffee. 'And this time, darlin', can you add another spoon of the instant?'

The fat old lady behind the counter opened her fat little mouth as if she might say something to defend the 'Filter Coffee' prices they were charging. 'And I'll have some more toast,' he snapped as he walked back to his table. She pinched her red lips.

It was 6am. His client was late. The greasy spoon was empty, bar a few cab drivers and a couple of homeless guys sheltering from the black, damp morning, nursing a weak mug of tea. The occasional bus rumbled down the Euston Road, the sleepy faces of passengers on the upper level obscured by their breath against the windows. Swift leafed through his file, rubbing his fingers against his palms nervously, thinking of the cheque he was about to receive. The largest he'd ever received in his career. Certainly not the last; not with all he'd learned... and not just about Alwynn...

The door opened and a rush of cold air whipped at the waitresses apron as she slammed down his mug of coffee. The homeless men ignored the well-dressed woman brushing the damp air from her overcoat.

'Mr Swift?' She slid into the opposite seat, an almost amused expression on her face. 'I believe you have a file for me? Oh, is that it?' She reached forward.

'Not so quickly...' he snatched the folder toward him. 'I think it would be fair to discuss the ... invoice first?'

She laughed quietly. 'Of course. But if your 'invoice' includes any of the nonsense you discussed on the phone last night... let me be clear: we had an agreement, Mr Swift.'

Jay was feeling a little unsettled; he hadn't expected her to be quite so ... strong. 'Look Mrs Jeffreys. You hired me to find Clive Alwynn. I had no idea why, and I certainly wouldn't have asked,' he bowed his head a little. 'However, now I *do* know why... and that changes things considerably. Including the invoice.'

'I really didn't think you'd be silly enough to get involved in ... what's the word I'm looking for? Extortion? No, that's far too harsh... I know - 'blackmail'. Such a nasty word, don't you think? You came to me on the 'recommendation' of a friend whose 15-year-old daughter had been raped. You helped to discredit the girl's character? Ahhh yes, you know who I'm talking about?

The CPS wouldn't prosecute on the grounds that the girl 'regularly participated in sex sessions with older men'. Your reports were rather lurid – but very convincing. The man in question – the rapist – he was a friend of yours, wasn't he? Seems he's still into children...' Swift looked confused. 'Yes,' she smiled coldly. 'A friend of ours is with the Special Branch.'

Swift was sweating now. He swigged his coffee. 'During my investigations... in the course of my observation of Clive Alwynn... I've stumbled upon so much more. So much that I feel compelled to share with you. And, of course, I've spent much more time and energy than we had originally...'

'I won't be taken for a fool, Mr Swift. I'm not interested in anything other than the original request. God knows we've already paid you so much... I think the original settlement is still more than fair.'

Swift's lip curled into a snarl. 'Listen lady, I don't know who you think you're dealing with, but...'

'No!' she banged her hand onto the table, silencing the waitress's chat with the taxi driver. 'You don't have any idea who *you're* dealing with, Swift. I know you know of my husband, but did you know his company owns the building where you've made your office?'

She smiled as the memory came back to him. 'Yes. Remember? – I told you I knew of a small place that might help you? Great thing about being a landlord is that you have a key to all property you own...' She watched the blood drain from his face, and she sighed. 'As I told you last night: I want the file on Clive Alwynn. I'm not interested in the other stuff. I've already seen lots of it, and it looks like just another chance for you to extort money.' She opened her bag and passed him the payment. 'Take it or leave it, Swift. I'm not the type to muck about.'

He smiled nastily, trying to recover. 'I can see that. OK. Here's the file.' She reached out quickly, just as he held it back. 'But do me one favour?'

She stared at him impassively.

He picked up the cheque and slipped it into his jacket, looking around nervously. 'Please,' and he slipped his business card into her hand. 'If you do get to meet Alwynn, give him my number? Please. Tell him I know about Palmer.'

She crumpled the card slowly, dropped it into his nearly empty coffee mug, turned and hurried out into the first grey light of dawn.

Swift unfolded the card and tried to smooth out the wrinkles, signalling for the waitress to top up his coffee. He stared down at the table and chewed his lip a little. Who was Polly Jeffreys? And if she had friends in the Special Force, why had she hired Jay Swift to track down Clive Alwynn? His day may have started badly, but things were beginning to look interesting again.

CHAPTER 32

The next morning, Nicole took William's car and headed for the farm. The meeting with the Trustees had gone smoothly enough – in fact, she'd liked them much more than she thought she would. It would have been easy to dismiss them as local pensioners wanting company, but they were much more than this: these people were fighting to construct a record of a way of living that had almost disappeared. Their pasts. Sure, this past had been hard – you could see it in every careworn line of their faces – but listening to their stories, seeing how easily they laughed, you could see that this past had been fulfilling, too. Several of them had known the Parnell family, and Nicole was relieved to see that any stigma attached to Elizabeth's liaison was confined to Emily Previs' imagination.

She had visited Little's and, confused by the vast selection of cakes, had asked the baker's wife to recommend one.

'Oh yes,' smiled the woman, her huge floury cheeks puffing up into a smile. 'Are you that girl that's visiting Emily Previs?'

'Well, yes, as a matter of fact, I am!'

'Right. Yes, she phoned this morning. She said you'd be collecting the strawberry cream double layer...'

Emily Previs was peering through the window as Nicole drove up.

'Come in, come in!' she shouted, gesturing to the back door and disappearing.

The kettle was bubbling away on the wood stove, and the table had been laid for morning tea.

'Hello Mrs Previs!' Nicole smiled and lay the boxed cake on the sideboard. 'How are you today? I collected the strawberry cream for you...'

'Yes, yes, good! I hope that Mrs Little didn't overcharge you – you being from London and all...'

'No, I don't think so.'

'My son came by last night,' said Emily eagerly, pouring the boiled water into the teapot.

'Oh yes? What did he think of the idea of the book, then?'

'Oh, he's very excited!' she smiled, stirring the teapot. 'He thinks it's a very good idea!'

Nicole laughed. 'Really? What did he say? What did you tell him?'

'Well,' said the old lady, gesturing to Nicole to pour. 'He says there might be an opportunity for us here, if we play it right.'

Nicole's heart sank. 'Look Mrs Previs, this is an academic book – it will never be a best-seller and in terms of sales, it will make very little money, at this stage I haven't even signed a contract...'

'Oh, shush, girl! And call me Emily, now that we're working together. No. You see, Alfred's daughter and her husband have a little B&B just the other side of the hill there. She's always dreamed of making more of it – maybe a little tearoom or something. Anyhow, Alfred says that if people hear about the poetry, they might want to come here and see the farm, and they'd stay at the B&B...'

'Right,' Nicole smiled. 'But Emily – I can't promise you that Elizabeth will be as popular as the Brontes.'

'I don't care about them. Alfred says as long she's as famous as those sisters over in Keighley, we'll have a decent business for his daughter. Now pass me that box there – no, that one. Yes, now I want you to see this. These are letters from Elizabeth's mother to Elizabeth... her husband had forbidden her to write, but she asked one of the farm hands to take them to her. Oh, he took them alright – and gave them straight back to the father. Poor woman. She never understood why the girl didn't answer her...'

Nicole unfolded the delicate pages, as Emily stood up to clear. 'Oh, let me help you...'

'No!,' said Emily. 'There's so much to do today – you read those. And then there's some stuff in the barn...'

A few hours later, Nicole had loaded three boxes of letters, documents and booklets into the Volvo. She'd take them back to London and – maybe – she'd find Elizabeth. She pictured Sebastian's delight when he saw the boxes on the lounge room floor, and the joy in his tail as he dived into the pages. She shuddered: thoughts of home. She sighed as the Volvo's lights cut across the bleak, Derbyshire hillsides.

CHAPTER 33

Sophie Géroux watched Clive's blue hire car wind up the drive.

She wiped her hands on the dishcloth and hurried out to greet him. 'Monsieur Alwynn!' She cried, embarrassed by her relief to see this young Englishman. Her husband was upstairs with Monsieur Feldmann, closing his curtains against the daylight. Monsieur had slept heavily since his collapse. The doctor visited twice a day, but during his waking hours, Gustav seemed as coherent as ever, she told him.

Once, she and her husband had talked of having children – but the chance had never arrived. She looked at Clive's strong arms and the way he held himself so confidently... maybe her son would have been like this? But he looked tired...

'How was your flight?'

'Fine, thank you, Madame Géroux.'

As they entered the hall, Géroux appeared.

'Ah, Monsieur Alwynn. Welcome. Monsieur Feldmann is deep in sleep – it's the drugs...'

'I thought it was a stroke...'

'No. Exhaustion. Stress. And Monsieur Feldmann has suffered with cancer for this past year.'

'Oh. He didn't say...'

'Please, let me take your bag up… Would you like your meal to be served in the lounge or the dining room?'

'Actually, Monsieur, would you mind if I joined you and your wife for a meal? I think… I don't…I think I need to…'

'Monsieur Alwynn,' Sophie Géroux placed her small hand on his forearm. 'George and I would be honoured. Please. Dinner will be in an hour or so, if that is suitable? Perhaps you would like to rest for a while?'

Clive was suddenly exhausted. He wanted to be held, to be warmed. He thought about Nic and looked to his dead mobile. No signal in the hills. And he was afraid to call her, afraid of what she might tell him. Maybe she and Michael were laughing now, happy at their second chance? He shuddered.

'That would be wonderful, Madame…'

'Please, call me Sophie.'

'And, please – Clive. That would be wonderful Sophie.'

Upstairs, he leaned down to stroke the dogs stretched in front of Gustav's bedroom door – depressed guardians. He could hear Gustav's laboured breathing through the slightly open door.

Clive showered quickly, and fell onto the bed. 'Nic!' he felt a deep pain, something he couldn't give words to. 'Oh, Nic…'

She'd never been his. How had he ever imagined she might be? He was destined to be alone. It had been so different when they first got together. That feeling of being alone –

that aloneness – seemed to evaporate the first time they'd made love. He'd known nothing about her at that moment, but after, laying together as the morning came up, he knew – thought he'd known – that he'd never be alone again.

How could she have kept the baby thing from him? Why didn't she consider him close enough to share that information? She was keeping him out.

Clive found people baffling in their self-containment. As a child, he'd tried so many times to reach out to people, to break through the shells they carried about them. But he'd never known how to. And in the end, people grew tired of his efforts and moved quietly away. Eventually, he developed a shell of his own, and lived in the same solitary space as everyone else.

He fell into a deep sleep.

Sophie Géroux stirred the casserole; she was glad they could offer their guest a proper meal. He'd looked tired and worn. And … lost, she thought.

Clive knocked at the door just after 7, and she smoothed the blouse she'd changed in to.

'Clive,' she smiled. 'Please! Come in. George is walking the dogs – he won't be long.'

'Thank you, Sophie. The dogs seemed rather down…'

'Down?'

'Oh, sorry – depressed.'

'Oh, yes. Believe it or not, they are sensitive creatures. It took many months for them to deal with Madame's passing. I am not sure which burdened them most: Madame passing or Monsieur's sadness.'

'It must have been difficult.'

'Ah, oui,' she sighed, gesturing him to take a seat at the laid table. 'It was such a dark time. They were so in love, Clive. Monsieur was not the same after that. George and I often say that it was the dogs that helped him through – he'd never wanted them, you see. But Madame was stubborn. It was as if she knew he would need them one day. She exhausted him with her begging!'

'Oh,' Clive laughed quietly. 'My sons wore me down, too – they demanded I get them a dog! And now we have Bella.'

'Bella? What a lovely name…'

'Yes; she eats us out of house and home, but my wife would be lost without her.'

'Ah, so she supported their sons in their quest?' Sophie smiled, stirring a little more red wine into the pot.

'Oh, no – Nicole is my second wife.'

'Oh, I'm sorry – I …'

'No – that's fine. The boys' mother – Virginia – moved to New York three years ago; she took the boys with her. And no – she didn't approve of the dog!'

'You must miss them so, your boys?'

'Yes – I do. But I think I've only just realised how much. I visited them in New York last week. They've grown so much. I feel I'm missing everything; missing their lives. I'm hoping they'll come and stay with me in London soon.'

'Your wife – does she – do you have children also?'

'No – she – we – to be honest, we're both too busy. And I don't know if I want...'

'Ah, I understand,' smiled Sophie, tapping the spoon against the rim of the casserole dish. 'George and I often thought about children, but – in the end, we were happy as we were, as we are. Just us. And yes, we also are busy. Life seems to rush through one's hands so quickly, doesn't it? Monsieur once told me that while his son was alive, time moved at least ten times more quickly than before. He was so desperate to capture every second of it...'

'Oh, I didn't realise Gustav had....'

'Yes. Thierry. We never knew him... he was from Monsieur's first marriage. He was only six.'

'God. How terrible. How did it...'

'A boating accident. The boy and his mother were away with friends. The sea was rough and the child fell overboard. It all happened very quickly – the mother never recovered from the shock. She passed not long after. Suicide.'

'Dear God....' Clive whispered. 'Poor Gustav.'

'Yes. He withdrew from the world for a long time. Madame told me that when she met him – at a friend's dinner party - he was totally alone. Not just physically, but also in his spirit. She said there was nothing to do but save him. She found her 'raison d'etre' that night, she said.'

Her husband shuffled through the door, the dogs, subdued, made their way up to their master's bedroom.

'I shall check on Monsieur, and join you in a moment. Sophie, please ensure our guest is looked after!'

'I am fine, thanks George. Your wonderful wife has looked after me well.'

After dinner, they stayed seated at the kitchen table; the wood fire stove burning down to embers.

Clive sighed. 'Sophie. Thank you for the meal. I can't remember the last time I've eaten so well.'

Sophie blushed at the compliment. 'Oh, thank you, Clive. It has been lovely to play hostess - and to such a charming man!'

'Wife!' smiled George. 'Mind yourself! You see the problem with marrying a good looking woman, Clive? You must always keep an eye on them!'

They all laughed, and Sophie, still blushing, busied herself with clearing the table. 'Will you have coffee, Clive?'

'No – thank you, I think it's time I slept. You say Gustav's most lucid in the early morning? I'd like to speak to him. See what he has planned – how he wants to deal with Walter.'

'Walter!' George banged his hand on the table. 'That man has always been a burden to Monsieur. He is a filthy human being! Forgive me Sophie, but that is the truth. Do you know, Clive, he had the nerve to call us yesterday and pretend to ask after Monsieur's health... but it was more a question of whether or not Monsieur would be fit enough to attend the Board meeting!'

'What Board meeting?' Clive frowned.

'It seems Walter has called an 'extra-ordinary' – is that the term? - meeting in Geneva. One week from now. He says that with Alonso's passing – ' Sophie crossed herself discreetly '- and Monsieur in such poor health, he must make some crucial decisions.'

Clive laughed mirthlessly. 'Yes, I see. Well, I'll do all I can, but I don't know if that will be helpful.'

'Monsieur has a lot of faith in you, Clive. Now, if you will excuse me, I need to have a last look around outside...'

Sophie frowned. 'But cherie, the dogs are settled, non?'

'Not the dogs, Madame. On my way back up the hill this evening, I saw something... maybe it was nothing, but...'

'What?' Clive frowned.

'I thought I saw a man standing at the end of the drive.'

'But who would that be? At that time of night... and why did they not come in?' asked Sophie.

'I'm not sure,' said George, taking the shotgun from the cupboard by the door. 'I'm sure it's nothing. I will see you in a moment.' And he walked out into the night.

Sophie wiped a damp cloth across the table, and dragged the screen to the front of the fire.

'Perhaps I should go with him?' said Clive.

'Oh, no, Clive! He often takes the gun – we have wild dogs up here... they sometimes confront Angel and Blue.'

'Alright, then. I'll wish you goodnight, Sophie.'

CHAPTER 34

The phone kicked straight into ansaphone. 'Hello? Clive?'
Virginia's clipped Counties accent echoed through the house.
'Clive? Are you there? ... Call me, will you? Ben's gone – he's
taken Jack – Rachel says they've gone to London, fucking
crazy woman – they're trying to get to you – God – '

Nicole grabbed the phone. 'Virginia?'

'God – um – hi, Nicole? – God. I don't know what to do. Is
Clive there?'

'No, he's – uh – he's away – '

'I am so bloody pissed off. Apparently, Clive signed them into
the Junior Flyer programme last time he was here, so Rachel
didn't need any parental consent ...'

'What? So they can just fly off without an adult – '

'I don't fucking know! Rachel – my nanny – is very calm. She
says everything's sorted. I'll bloody kill her! I'm so close to
calling the police. Do you know how many years you get for
kidnapping over here?'

'No, I don't,' said Nicole as a wave of nausea swept through
her. So much for Cyn's hair of the dog; she'd simply given her
another hangover!

'Well, they're either kidnapped or landing at Heathrow as we
speak – I'm just *so* pissed off!'

'Yeah – yes – um – what time is the flight due?'

'11.40...'

'OK, look – I'll go to Heathrow – um – I'll call you if they're
here – um – '

'I'm just *so* pissed off – '

'I know! You said that – ' Nicole reached for the vase and
threw up violently.

'I'm sorry – I'm so scared...' Virginia's voice broke.

'I know – I'll call you – my mobile's on – do you have my
number?'

She called a mini-cab, hastily brushed her teeth and changed
into jeans and jumper. She could fix her makeup in the cab.

The journey seemed to take an eternity, no thanks to the
driver's chatting. 'So. Off on holiday? Or going to meet your
husband – lucky man!' And he laughed suggestively.

Nicole forced smiles, but gave him very little information.

'You want I should wait?' he asked when they reached the
airport.

'No,' she said. 'That'll be fine. Put it on our account.' And she
walked away, ignoring his curses.

She scanned the arrivals board; there it was. Landed on time,
about 30 minutes ago. With any luck they were just coming
through the gate.

She stood behind the gathered crowd, her heart flipping a little every time the doors slid open. What if they weren't there? What if they weren't on the flight? What if this Rachel was a complete loon?

Suddenly, there they were. They stood hesitantly on the other side of the door so that it opened and closed a couple of times. They seemed to be immobilised, not sure of what to do next.

'Ben?!' She called. 'Jack?!'

They looked startled, and Ben pushed his brother a little, and they walked through the doors shyly.

'I'm Nicole,' she smiled. 'Daddy asked me to come and get you.'

'Where is he?' Jack asked suspiciously.

'Away on business. Come on, Bella's waiting for us. You remember Bella don't you?'

Ben nodded as she took Jack's backpack from him.

By the time they pulled up in the drive, it was well after 2am. The black cab journey back from Heathrow had been a long and silent ride.

Ben had nodded off and fallen into Jack's lap, while Jack glowered out into the rainy night. In profile, he had Clive's soft lips and determined chin, and the long up-turned eyelashes made her chest ache a little. But the round, button-like nose must have been Virginia's – Ben's was the same.

Bella danced about in the front window, then drew back, barking alarm at the sleepy boys dragging their bags up the front steps.

Ben woke suddenly and screeched 'Bella! Jack! Look! It's Bella!'

The boy rushed forward, but the dog ran away, and Sebastian, alarmed by the noise and activity, fled beneath the lounge.

'It's alright,' smiled Nicole. 'It's late, and they're not used to being up at this time of night…'

Bella stood in the kitchen doorway, cocking her head in confusion, watching them.

'Look Bella,' said Nicole. 'It's Ben and Jack!'

The dog sniffed cautiously and then her tail swung into happy recognition – or at least acceptance.

'Right,' smiled Nicole, relieved. 'Let's get your beds sorted out and then we'll have something to eat…'

'We ate on the plane.' said Jack.

'I'm hungry…' whispered Ben to Jack.

'Well, let's see what we've got in the fridge,' smiled Nicole, realising the chances of child-friendly food, any food, were slim. Nothing but tomato juice and vodka.

Jack was already upstairs; she imagined she heard him stop in shock as he turned on his bedroom light and saw that it was now a study.

'Oh – Jack?' She ran upstairs. 'We made an office, but look – we kept this room for when you visited.'

She flung open the door to reveal a larger room, with two beds and a bookcase, and shelves full of toys all hopelessly too young. Clive had meant well – had created a room that his sons would have loved when they were two or three years younger. But now it looked more like a shrine, and both beds carried a deep circle of Sebastian's fur. She rushed forward to turn the radiator on.

The boys looked at one another doubtfully and threw their bags on to the beds. She went back downstairs to try and find anything edible. She didn't know whether to feel anger or relief as Jack crawled into the cupboard under the stairs and emerged with cans of spaghetti hoops and baked beans with sausages. My God, how long had they been there? Why didn't Clive ever mention it, or, better still, why hadn't he cleared them out?

Jack noticed her confusion. 'Mommy always leaves the cans under there. There's plenty more.'

'Right,' she laughed nervously. 'Well, I've got toast, at least. I think...'

Ben clapped his hands; 'Hooray! Jack found spag hoops!'

She was staring out into the garden, resting her weight against the sink. She was exhausted. Where was Clive? She saw Jack's pale, expressionless reflection in the window.

'Do you know how to cook them?' he gestured toward the tin.

She turned, feigning a smile. 'Maybe. I'm not much of a cook, I'm afraid.'

'My Mom's a *great* cook!' He looked suddenly angry, fierce.

'Well maybe next time you'll bring her with you...' she said under her breath. She opened the tin, and Sebastian leapt up onto the sideboard hopefully.

'Get down Sebastian! Look, Jack. Let's eat, have a wash and get some sleep. Daddy will be back soon and everything will be alright.'

She'd call him as soon as the boys were in bed.

'I don't care when he gets back,' Jack said sulkily.

'Don't say that, Jack. I know you want to see Daddy...'

'I don't!' he shouted.

'Oh, really?' she slammed the microwave door closed. 'So *that's* why you and Ben flew all the way from New York?'

'Ben wanted to! I didn't! But I couldn't let him go on his own. Rachel said.'

'OK. Let's talk about it tomorrow. It's late now. Ben? Come and have some supper!'

She set the plates down on the breakfast bar, and buttered the toast.

Ben scrambled up onto a stool.

Jack was silent as he picked up the bowl and threw it against the kitchen wall. The spaghetti hoops stuck for a moment and then, dribbled away, fell away like rubbery leaves. Bella, after an initial scattering of surprise, ran to lick the carnage.

She watched the tension in his shoulders as he strode from the room. So much like Clive, she thought, reaching for the dishcloth. Damn it! She thought of the tins under the stairs. Damn it! Why hadn't he told her about the tins?

Ben ate silently, head down, occasionally stroking Bella with his foot as she passed suspiciously. Within minutes he had fallen forward onto the counter and sighed into sleep.

'Come on, Ben. Let's get you up to bed,' she whispered.

Once she'd turned their light out, she went downstairs to check for messages – nothing from Clive, but ten missed calls from Virginia. She poured herself a glass of wine and braced herself.

'Hi Virginia. It's Nicole. They're here now. Fast asleep and safe. Give me a call in the morning.'

Then she called Clive's mobile. 'Clive? Hi. I'm sorry I hurt you. Please believe me – I didn't mean to. I love you. Jack and Ben are here – don't worry, they're safe. I don't know if Virginia called you.... they ran away. Well – it seems their nanny, Rachel, put them on the plane... Oh, Clive... I need you. Please – don't give up on me?'

Through a haze of sleep, Nicole heard Bella growling downstairs. Panicking, she leapt out of bed and rushed down. It was 5am. Jack and Bella were rolling around the lounge room, fighting over a shoe – Clive's trainer. She watched as Jack laughed helplessly, occasionally tickling Bella's round belly. The dog's tail thrashed the floor with delight, and her eyes rolled back. 'Bella!', Jack laughed. 'You silly girl!'

'See!' she laughed. 'Bella remembers you!'

He stopped playing and stood up, awkwardly. 'What time is Daddy coming home?'

'Oh, um.... I don't know yet. He's on the road.... let's wait for his call. That's the way these business trips go...'

'Great. He knows we're here and he's too busy to come home?'

'No! No, Jack! It's not like that! Look, he went to France – I think his mobile doesn't work there....'

Jack raised his eyebrows sceptically.

'OK – I don't know. That's the answer, o.k? But I know if he knows you're here, he'll come home. OK?'

Jack turned away. 'Sure. What's for breakfast?'

'I don't know yet – um....'

But Jack had already disappeared into the cupboard under the stairs.

'One thing I do know,' she forced a smile. 'We're going to the shops after breakfast.'

Jack pulled his hoodie up over his head and hunched his shoulders forward. Ben talked non-stop and tangled himself in Bella and her leash, as the three of them walked to the supermarket.

'Do you remember any of this, boys?' Nicole shouted from behind them.

'No!' Ben cried happily. Jack said nothing.

They wandered the aisles, Nicole throwing tins into the trolley, while Jack read the labels –

'We can't have this – it's full of E-numbers....'

'Right,' she said. 'What shall we get then?'

'I don't know – what do you want to cook?'

'I told you – I'm not much of a cook....'

He sighed, feigning frustration. 'Look. If you can get some mince, and bread rolls, I can make burgers.'

Ben danced about. 'Yeah! Burgers! Nic, will Bella be alright? She's outside....'

'Yes,' Nicole smiled. 'She's tied to the dog ring... we won't be long. OK, Ben. Tell me what we need. We should get some salad, too? I've got orange juice at home, but do you want something else? I'm in your hands.....'

He almost smiled, but checked himself and read the label on the mince packs.

'My mom was right – food in this country sucks.'

The television was loud; the boys were huddled on the sofa, laughing at the cartoons. Bella sat right in front of them, eyeing their burgers and fries.

Nicole sat at the dining table behind them, watching the way they moved, the way they laughed, the way they turned their heads. There was certainly some Clive there – but something else, too. Virginia, no doubt, but something more – something like disappointment. And sadness. No ... with Jack it was more like bitterness.

He turned to her, still smiling, but his face froze when he saw her smiling at him.

'Have you had enough to eat,' she asked. He nodded.

'Ben? I think we better get you off to the bath in a minute.... you must be tired.'

He nodded sleepily.

After she tucked him in, she came back downstairs. Jack was sitting silently at the table.

'Well,' she said. 'Mummy said she's flying out tomorrow – tomorrow night our time. She's going to meet us at Heathrow. I wouldn't worry too much about her being cross.... she sounded relieved to me. I think she's more cross with Rachel.'

'It's not Rachel's fault,' he said quietly.

'I know. But don't worry. They'll sort it out.'

'Where's my dad?'

'Grenoble. He called this afternoon. I've tried to get through, but he's busy – the line's engaged all the time. And his mobile's dead.'

'What's he doing there?'

He followed her as she cleared the plates from the lounge floor and went to the kitchen. 'He's visiting a client – Gustav Feldmann. Daddy just won this amazing account – one of Europe's biggest banks.'

'One of the oldest, too.'

'Ah,' she smiled. 'Have you been checking up on him?' She poured a glass of wine.

'No I haven't!' He leaned down to ruffle Bella's coat. 'Are you and daddy going to have babies?'

She coughed on her wine – 'No! I mean - no. We talked about it – sort of – but neither of us really has the time.... and can you imagine Bella putting up with the competition?'

He smiled as Bella, hearing her name, whined and wagged her tail expectantly.

'I have to go to bed,' he said. 'Can I call mommy?'

'Sure!' she glanced at the kitchen clock. 'Use the kitchen phone – here...'

He rolled his eyes. 'I have my cell.'

'Right. I'll go upstairs... um.... I'll see you in the morning.'

He ignored her, concentrating on his phone.

'What are we doing tomorrow?' he asked, feigning disinterest.

'I think we'll go up to the Heath,' she said quickly, wondering why.

*****

Thank God the sun is shining, Nicole thought, as they trudged their way across the Heath.

Ben and Jack walked ahead; Ben dancing wildly with Bella, so it looked as though they were caught by the wind and twisting like Whirling Dervishes. They'd occasionally fall into Jack, and he'd push them away, churlishly, but without much conviction.

Even hidden within his hoodie, she knew he was watching Ben closely – and that he was observing her all the time.

It had been a rough night; Ben had woken so many times with various nightmares. Nicole eventually carried him downstairs and settled him on the couch. When she'd woken in the armchair at 2am, Bella and Ben were snuggled tightly together, sleeping soundly.

She imagined Jack had slept just as fitfully, but that he hid beneath the blankets, pretending not to hear.

They slept late and shared a quiet breakfast before setting out. There was still no word from Clive.

She found herself being thankful for the distraction of the boys; she imagined how terrible the night might have been had she been alone.

Ben called out: 'Look Nic! Look! Kites!' and he and Bella rushed up the hill where a group of men were swooping and swooshing their kites across the breathtaking views of London.

'Don't get lost!' she cried, aware that her words were blown back to her on the blustering wind. She ran forward, just behind Jack, struggling to keep up with them.

At the top of the hill, she fell onto a bench. Bella ran back to her, barking loudly and excitedly, urging her to come run with them.

'No, I'm too puffed,' she laughed. 'Yes! Isn't it exciting?'

Jack fell down beside her. 'She seems to remember him.'

'She remembers both of you – I haven't seen her so animated ever!' She laughed as Bella rolled onto her back. 'Belly tickles, is it? Ok, then!' And she tickled the big round belly until the dog cried out with delight and rushed away to join Ben.

One of the kite-flyers was chatting to Ben, offering the strings of his kite to him. Ben held them tentatively, and then was tugged forward as the sail lifted on the wind.

Nicole and Jack laughed loudly.

'God! We'd better be careful or he'll end up at Heathrow!'

'Maybe he'll lift off and fly past mommy's plane!' laughed Jack.

They passed an hour watching the kites slash through the air, Ben, Bella and now Jack, all dancing and running and swirling in the cold wind, their jackets flapping wildly, their pale faces flushed.

'Come on!' she called, when the men began to wind in their kites. 'Let's go and get warm!'

'Do we have to?' Ben called back to her.

'Yes! Come on – let's go home and get some dinner! Bella's exhausted!'

CHAPTER 35

Gustav listened to the wind; *high wind in the tall trees*. That was from a song, wasn't it? Sometimes, when the light fell across the mountains at the end of the day and he was alone in the bed, he stared out into the garden and he saw Carlotta there. *Carlotta!*

When she walked by the window she seemed distracted. She was looking down the fields, she was searching for him. For Thierry. She looked back to Gustav, brushing the waves of her hair from her face. She looked lost. *Carlotta!* he wanted to shout out. She smiled apologetically, then hurried forward down the hill.

Wind in the tall trees... he heard her shrieking: *Thierry! Thierry!*

He felt the pain in his back and fumbled for the button that released the morphine.

What had Lilli said? '*Bring them back, Gustav. Answer her...If she's calling to you, answer her. I won't mind.*'

'Yes Lilli,' he sighed as the pain fell away. 'Carlotta?' he called. 'Come back!'

He watched her stop and turn to him. She looked lost, desperate, her hands moved like trapped birds – she was searching for traces of their son – madly running her hands through the closing ripples of the waves that had taken him.

'He's not coming back, darling,' Gustav whispered, and he felt a stunted tear roll freely down the dry skin of his cheek. 'Lilli!'

He felt like he was shouting, but the dogs didn't stir and the fire still murmured in the grate. 'Lilli! Help her!'

Lilli bent forward and kissed his forehead.

He watched as Lilli caught Carlotta by the waist as she fell, and she pointed across the field. And then he saw the boy dancing wildly in the high winds, singing and happy as he'd always been.

CHAPTER 36

Palmer gathered the creative and sales teams around the large meeting room table. He'd sent an email the previous afternoon stating that attendance at tomorrow morning's 9am roundtable was compulsory. A frisson of surprise and muted outrage fluttered around the office – '9 o'clock? I was here 'til midnight last night, and probably will be again tonight...' But then laughter, to think that Palmer would even be awake by then, let alone dressed... or sober.

But there he was. Not exactly fresh-faced, but his shirt was pressed and his jacket unwrinkled. He'd called the meeting early, knowing that he only had a couple of hours to sort out the presentation for Geneva. He'd sent the invitation as late as possible the previous afternoon, knowing that Clive would have little time to react should any of the team try and warn him.

He poured himself a coffee and smiled at the expectant gathering. He sighed deeply.

'Thank you all for coming. I know you've all been working *so* hard on the Feldmann's account – creative is really starting to get there, and our video presentation to New York went down very well indeed....'

He ignored the designer's indignant glare. 'I think we're being let down a little by Sales, however. Simply *winning* the Feldmann's account must have raised interest in the financial supplement we're producing? And what about partnership deals for the site? Debs?' he turned sharply on his heel.

'Well,' she blushed, caught off-guard. 'Well, we've certainly had interest in the financial supplement, but Feldmann's have been very resistant to co-sponsors on their site ...'

'We're not offering *co-sponsorship*, Debs. We're looking for value-add organisations. What about that Pensions fund lot?'

Debs looked at him with undisguised loathing. 'Yes, well, I'm still talking to them... they should come back to us soon. Feldmann's seem ok with them...'

Palmer sighed again. 'I'm not sure,' he smiled at her '...you realise how urgent the situation is Debs,' and he turned to the sales guys and rolled his eyes. They snickered a little. 'I'm flying to Geneva this afternoon – I'd like to take a definite deal of some sort.'

'That's impossible,' she said flatly.

'Nothing's impossible for those who wish to keep their jobs, Debs.' And he stared at her coldly.

'So!' he looked around the room. 'It's all change from here on, team! We're all going to start working harder. I've developed a very good relationship with Feldmann, Walter Feldmann .... he seems to be a little more on the ball than Gustav. And James has asked me to take over the account for the foreseeable... so, no more slacking.'

A silent gasp hung in the air.

'And what about Clive?' the designer stared directly at Palmer.

'Oh, I'm sure Clive will be busy with... lots of other projects...
As soon as he's back from Geneva, we'll have him working
again!' And he laughed dismissively. 'So. What I'd like to do,
now, is to meet the lead of each team. I expect a complete,
up-to-date status report by, say, 12.30?'

'What about my Client meetings?' said one of the sales guys.

'Reschedule them.' And he snapped shut his notebook and
strode from the room.

The team looked to one another, but said nothing – that
would be later, after work.

Debs went back to her desk and logged onto her computer.

'So – what do you think about that?' Danny, a new junior
sales guy whispered.

'Not much,' she said dismissively. 'And stop looking down my
top, you pervert.'

The boy blushed and hurried away.

She checked her email – there it was in the Sent box.
Yesterday. 5.55. She'd forwarded Palmer's email missive to
Clive. He'd be interested to see that Palmer was taking the
lead on the Feldmann's account.

She smiled and deleted the forwarded message.

She put in a few calls to the Pensions people, and, by 2pm
she had enough information to shut Palmer up. She tossed

the dossier into his in-tray on her way out. 'I'm off to a Client meet,' she called to no one in particular.

But she had no Client meetings. She went to the seedy video store in Soho. A bored young man hardly looked up when she said she'd come to collect copies of *Asian Schoolgirl Sluts* and *Abused Beauties*. A couple of days before, she'd overheard Palmer calling Walter Feldmann's office. 'Of course,' he'd said. 'I'll meet you there.' She knew enough about the Feldmann's set-up to know that Walter was not the key contact, and she wondered why Palmer would set up such a meeting while Clive was in New York?

Over the next few days, she found several references to Walter Feldmann on the net – one, a newspaper article from last year, reporting that Feldmann had been taken to hospital 'after a fall' at his Swiss home. He was pictured with his 'devoted' wife Jenelyn by his side. Jenelyn looked young enough to be his daughter, and she was dressed like a hooker, Debs thought. A search on Jenelyn Feldmann led, eventually, to a link to films – pornography.

She loaded the dvd into the machine. Lurid, 1970s funk music blasted out loud, while a voice-over described the wantonness of young Phillipino girls. She turned her head to the side, trying to make sense of the naked bodies writhing on the screen.

'Oh my god,' she laughed, covering her mouth with one hand. 'That's disgusting!' She poured herself another glass of red. It was late, but she was determined to see this through. Truth was, she found it rather exciting in its sordidness.

She watched Jenelyn, who could have only been 14, writhing in fake pleasure as three, older Western men had their way with her. There were more 'stories', each one centring on Jenelyn's degradation at the hands of the fat, middle-aged men.

The films were directed by Walt Manfield, and produced by Geld Productions. She scribbled the words down on a pad, and began to play with them, while the DVD continued with its grunting and squealing.

She smiled, thankful for her high school German. *Manfield.* Feldmann. *Geld.* Money. Walter Feldmann was nothing but a rich pornographer and a paedophile. No wonder he and Palmer had teamed up.

'Goodness me,' she smiled to herself. 'I wonder if James knows exactly who Palmer is doing business with?' She emailed Clive.

To: *Clive.Allwynn@AdVerbe.com*
From: *Deborah.Curtis@btinternet.com*

Hi Clive,

I hope you got the email I forwarded yesterday? We had a jolly meeting with Palmer this morning. It seems he's teamed up with Walter Feldmann. I imagine you know nothing about this... Well, our man Walter is a very interesting fellow.

I've attached some background on him, and some stuff about the film company he runs. I've watched a few of his 'films' tonight, and they are not for the faint-hearted. Interestingly,

Walter's company is under investigation in the States. Drug connections, apparently.

Anyway, I suppose you might wonder why I'm doing this? Let's just say I don't like to see the good guys get screwed. And I don't like Palmer. I'm sure that's something we have in common? :-)

Let me know if you need any more – but please use this private email account, or call me at home. Maybe it's just paranoia, but I have a feeling I'm being watched at the office – I don't know... just a few strange things have happened.

Deborah

CHAPTER 37

Nicole wiped Ben's nose, kneeling down to sort out the straps of his backpack.

'I promise Ben – Sebastian will remember you when you come back! And look! There's Bella!' She waved his phone in front of him.

'Daddy is sorry he missed you! But it will only be a month – and then you'll be here again. Or maybe five weeks… We have to do it properly. Make plans. Daddy and Mummy are going to talk about all these things!'

Jack half-smiled at her; she met his eyes. 'I can't wait to see you both again; I can't wait to get to know you. And I told you – Daddy cried when I told him you were at home. He wanted to fly back straight away. But Gustav is dying – remember? The old man who owns the bank…'

'Well, the old man who's *in charge for the moment…..,*' Jack corrected her.

'Whatever,' she pretended to frown. 'The old man's moment is about to end. Daddy's got to fight his corner, boys. And then he's coming back here and getting ready to see you again. That's what men have to do sometimes…'

Ben smiled a little. 'Is Daddy like a soldier?'

'Yes,' said Jack, putting his arm around Ben. 'Daddy's a soldier.'

Nicole smiled at him, and marvelled at how much she was going to miss them.

Virginia's cut-glass tone tore across the space.

'Jack! Ben!'

She raced forward to embrace them.

'Mommy!' They shouted in unison.

She held them tightly, finally catching sight of Nic standing awkwardly behind them.

She stood up quickly.

'You must be Nicole? Hi – look – I can't thank you enough… I see Clive's not here? Of course…' She stroked Jack's shoulder. 'Anyway – must let you go – the traffic back to our place – sorry – your place… is bad at this time. Tell Clive I'll call.'

'Yes, I'll tell him. And Virginia, Clive *will* be seeing the boys soon – we're hoping they'll be here for the summer. Even a couple of weeks. It would be good for them all.'

Virginia's jaw clenched a little. 'Well – we'll discuss that with our lawyers, won't we boys?' She laughed a hollow, crystal laugh. 'Anyway, come on! The car's waiting. Grandma and Poppy are waiting for us – ' She looked to Nicole. 'My parents are waiting for us and it's a long drive to Hampshire.'

'Sure. Good to see you boys.'

As the three of them walked away, Jack looked back once, and she imagined the bitterness had gone. Ben turned back and gave a jaunty salute, like the soldier he was.

She laughed out loud, and they disappeared through the Heathrow crowds. How would she have survived the last few days without them?

CHAPTER 38

Nicole pulled into the drive around 5.30, still thinking of the boy's farewell. The front light was on, and the lamps in the lounge. Clive... her heart was pounding as she turned the key in the lock. 'Clive?' She called out, and Bella ran at her, a huge, lumbering ball of joy. 'Hello Bella... where's daddy?'

Clive was sitting in the lounge.

'Honey,' she whispered. 'When did you get back?' She fell onto the lounge beside him. She looked up, hoping he'd kiss her. He brushed her hair back from her forehead, smiled and said 'Just now. Virginia left me a message to say she'd collected the boys from the airport? What the fuck happened? How did it happen? Imagine them travelling halfway around the world on their own? How were they?'

She laughed quietly and touched his face gently. 'It's alright. Everything is fine, darling. Let me take my coat off and I'll tell you everything. Have you eaten?'

Clive stood up quickly. 'Yes. I... look, I'm exhausted. I imagine I'll take a shower and get some sleep... if that's ok. Tell me about the boys while I unpack?'

She watched him leave the room, and she wanted to stroke the knotted muscles of his shoulders. But she knew he'd pull away from her touch. For the moment, he was gone from her. She pushed down the urge to cry out to him, and rubbed at her stomach as if she could smooth away the wave of acid that was burning her from the inside out.

CHAPTER 39

Clive looked around the bar; the lights were low – neon,
purple – and Australian and New Zealand accents rose above
the thump of the house music blaring through the tinny
speakers. 'Perfect,' he thought. 'The ideal place for Palmer's
cronies.'

Swift had called him again, the day before: 'My client is willing
to meet with you - to discuss a sensitive matter.' And he'd
mentioned Clive's mother's name. 'Listen, you little shit,' Clive
had hissed over the phone. 'I don't respond well to this sort of
shit - I know Palmer's behind this.... you tell him....' Swift
hung up.
Now, sitting at the bar, whiskey in his hand he waited. A tall,
blonde woman, far too well-dressed for this dive searched the
crowd. She seemed to stop when she saw him. She walked
forward tentatively, pushing aside a drunken South African.
'Mr Allwyn?' she tried to smile and held out her hand, but then
withdrew it. 'Clive?'

'Who the fuck are you? And what the hell is going on?'

She watched the vein in his neck rise with anger – just like his
father's. And she fought the impulse to smooth back his hair.
'Clive,' she reached forward and rested a hand on his forearm,
just before he shook it off. 'Clive. Let's get out of here, please.
Give me a chance to explain?'

Outside, she hailed a taxi. 'The Criterion,' she said to the
driver. And as she fell back into her seat, he saw in the
harshness of the streetlights that she was in her late fifties;
tired looking, but also kind. He couldn't begin to understand

why a woman like her would have any dealings with someone as revolting as Palmer.

'What's going on?' he asked when the waiter had shown them to their table.

'Whiskey,' she smiled to the waiter. 'Jamieson's.'

'Oh,' he smiled unpleasantly. 'Swift raided our bottle recycling as well, did he?'

She laughed gently. 'Probably. But I hope he didn't invoice me for that.'

Clive was incredulous at her calm, but struggled to keep control of the conversation. 'Can I at least ask your name?'

'Of course, sorry. That was rude of me. I'm Polly. Polly Jeffreys.'

Clive frowned, running through the 'Jeffreys' he'd ever met – 'I don't know any... why are you...'

'I'm married to Robert Jeffreys,' she said, as though it might mean something to him.

'Who the fuck is Robert Jeffreys? Is he working with Palmer? Look can we just get to the point here, please? I don't know about you, but I've had just about enough of this as I can take, and, please 'Polly', you probably already know this, but I am known to lose my temper occasionally.'

She wanted to laugh; laugh with delight, with relief. If she'd ever doubted that Clive Allwyn was Robert's son – she knew now. This was his boy. That lost piece of his life that had rested like a bruise in his side for the last 40 years. 'Polly,' he'd told her when the doctors had told him he had no more than six months to live. 'Polly? I'm not afraid of dying. I'm afraid of leaving you, I'm afraid of leaving the kids. But I'm most afraid of leaving things unfinished, Poll.'

She hadn't understood, but holding him in her arms that night, trying not to imagine a world without him, he'd kissed her gently on the forehead and told her about another son – his first son.

'It was a terrible time, Poll. Mandy was a write-off, the kids were running amok, the business had gone bust. I took them down to the seaside – I was young then. Stupid. Thought the sea would cure us all. A cure, Poll, that's what I was looking for. But I knew it was all over. I felt... dead, I suppose. There was a young girl there. Nothing special. But she talked to me ... I ended up sleeping with her. Oh, Poll...'

And he cried into the night, until finally they'd slept.

Now, sitting in the gold light of The Criterion, impossibly handsome waiters circling the room, she looked across the table. 'Clive,' she said. 'I'm married to your father.'

She watched his expression change from anger to impatience to fear in a moment. He tried to speak, but no words came out.

'Clive,' she tried to smile, but felt the tears she'd fought all evening welling up. 'Clive, please. I need to tell you about him – Robert. He's a great man.'

'Right,' Clive was struggling to keep a handle on things. 'That'd be the great man who knocked up a 14-year-old and then left her and his kid to it?'

'I know. On the surface it looks bad,' she cringed at just how bad it looked. 'He tried to find you Clive, I swear, but your mother's father must have intercepted the letters. If you…'

'If I what? Why now? That's what I'm interested in. Now. Why?'

'You're so much like him, Clive. He doesn't dwell in the past, either.'

'Stuff this,' he cried, banging his glass down. 'What I want to know is why he exposed me and my wife to the likes of someone like Swift? What's in it for him, Polly?'

Polly sighed. 'He doesn't know I'm doing this. He'd be furious. He'd slam down his whiskey, say 'What the fuck?' a lot, and walk out before I had a chance to explain.'

Clive sat back in his chair, and smiled a little despite himself. 'And what would you tell him, Polly? What would make him stay and give a shit for the story you were about to tell him.'

She smiled, sensing the victory. 'Well, let's get another drink, and I'll tell you everything.'

CHAPTER 40

Virginia gathered the boys about her and hurried out of the airport to the waiting car.

Jack seemed fearful, holding back.

'Is Rachel here?' asked Ben.

'No. Damn right she isn't.' Virginia shot a quick look to Jack, and then softened her voice. 'No. She's back at home, looking after Mr Porky.'

The driver gathered the boys' backpacks and Virginia's suitcase and loaded them into the boot.

'Where are we going?' ventured Jack, not looking his mother in the eye, as the car pulled away.

'To Gran and Grandpa's.'

'How long will it take?'

'Oh, a couple of hours. I imagine you're tired? Sleep.'

Ben fidgeted with the dvd screen in the back of the seat in front of him. 'Bella slept with me. Do you remember Sebastian, mummy?'

Virginia picked up the change in his accent. 'Of course,' she smiled tightly. '*Mommy* remembers it all.'

Ben laughed. 'Sebastian is fat, but not as fat as Mr Porky. Nic says that she has to fight him when he tries to get Bella's food!'

Jack interjected. 'She doesn't know how to cook. She made us spaghetti from under the stairs.'

Virginia tried not to look too smug, but then remembered the current circumstances. 'If you EVER do this to me again, Jack. I swear...'

He saw the tears well up in her eyes and gently touched her arm. 'I won't Mommy.'

They arrived in Hampshire not long after lunch. Virginia's parents hurried out into the drive. Her mother was clearly overwhelmed.

'Darling!' She rushed forward, awkwardly, grasping her daughter's neck. Virginia pushed her away and planted a small kiss on her cheek. 'Hello mother. Pappa!' She rushed forward and hugged the frail old man. 'How are you?'

The driver unloaded the bags into the drive, and Virginia's father hobbled forward to collect them.

'No! Daddy! Don't!' Virginia leaned in front of him and grabbed the bags. 'Boys? Please bring in the bags for Granpa.'

'No, don't worry darling,' he smiled fondly. 'Mr O'Reilly is here with us today...' A sun-beaten man, in his mid-40s bounced down the drive. 'Miss Grey!' He grabbed the bags from the boys and smiled across at her.

'Mr O'Reilly?' Virginia looked confused.

He laughed. 'The son of Mr O'Reilly. I think the last time we met we were about 12? I'm Stephen.'

'Ah,' she smiled, despite herself. 'How are you Stephen? And it's Mrs Alwynn now,' she hated the way she had that knee-jerk reaction to her name.

'Right. Is that right?' Stephen looked bemused by her abruptness. 'Come on boys!' he gestured to Ben and Jack. 'Shall I show you your room? And the swimming pool? I hear you can't swim, you poor American boys?'

'Can too!' said Jack angrily.

'Well, then, you're going to have to show me!' And he winked at Virginia. Jesus, she thought, trying to force a smile. We are all getting old. She recalled long summer days in the pool with Stephen O'Reilly – the gardener's son.

Stephen and the boys raced into the house.

'My God!' she said to her parents. 'I don't know where they get the energy from!'

Her father laughed. 'Ah, boys... they are boys.'

As they settled in the pristine kitchen, its 1970s décor unchanged, her mother began fussing with tea and biscuits. Her father tried to help, but he simply got in the way. Virginia was shocked at how much they'd aged while she'd been away.

Her mother, Rose, had been a glamorous housewife of the early 1960s. She'd led a cliched life; married young, straight out of college (typing, cooking, book-keeping and mother-craft). She'd married Gordon when she was 18. Looking at her now, Virginia was begrudgingly impressed by her mother's ability to maintain her appearance; sure, she was older, but her hair was perfectly cut, coloured and tied back in a loose bun. Her clothes were immaculate; a tailored trouser-suit that skimmed over her flat bottom, and breathed out and gave room to her small, rounded-belly. If only her mother had used her skills at a *real* job, she thought. She'd have been a Managing Director so fast! Instead, she'd frittered away her talents baking cakes and making jams.

Her father was the son of a moderately wealthy man, and had been set to inherit the family business when his father died. Grey's was a successful hardware business that expanded from a small, village shop to a vital outlet for the developers who were eating their way into the countryside, fulfilling the increasing need for modern, affordable housing. When the Internet explosion happened, Clive had the great idea of greysonline.com, an online delivery service for builders. Gordon Grey sold the company and retired with more money than he or his father could have ever hoped for.

Watching him shuffling about the kitchen, behind his wife, in his M&S trousers and casual shoes, Virginia was sad to see that he was a few inches shorter than she remembered him. He seemed disoriented, a little distracted. He looked over to her occasionally and she wasn't entirely sure he knew who she was.

As usual, her mother chuffed and huffed and chided and talked non-stop; yes, Mrs Bramson's son was divorced, too;

yes, Rebecca Taylor had died last year, cancer, so poor Robert was on his own with the girls (36 and 42); Jonnie Holston was in rehab again, his poor wife!

Virginia cut across the prattle: 'So where's Mr O'Reilly? Stephen's father? And, mummy, I think I'd rather a gin and tonic…' She saw her mother's tight-mouthed disapproval. 'I think I'm still on US time….'

'Oh really?' her mother replied, not looking up from the plate of biscuits she was arranging. 'So, they start drinking in the morning in America, do they?'

Her father spoke up, not daring to look at his wife. 'Me too, in fact! Let's go through to the lounge and settle in…'

'But the boys?' Virginia said.

'They're with Stephen – they're fine. Rose, will you come through with us?'

But his wife was already pulling out pots and pans. 'Those poor boys!' she cried. 'No. I'll cook some lunch… well it's so late now, I guess it's supper… No, you two go.'

They fell back into the lounge chairs by the French doors that opened onto the immaculate lawns rolling down to the pool house. Virginia laughed as the boys – already in their swimming costumes - ran by, squealing and laughing as Stephen O'Reilly chased them with a small bucket of water. 'Come back you little Yanks! I'll teach you to splash an Irishman!'

'His father?' she asked.

'Oh, poor old Jack passed away a couple of years ago, now.'

'Oh, how sad...'

'Well, he'd been ill for a long time. Stephen started picking up some of his father's regular appointments when he was home from Uni on the summer holidays, and in the end he just took on the business.'

'Oh, no. What a waste of a University education...'

'Gin, honestly! That education of yours has made you quite the snob!' he said gently, but with an edge. 'Stephen studied horticulture. His business is landscape design – his company's just done the grounds of the new art gallery. Beautiful job. I think he likes to keep his hand in, though, and he's pleased we need the help here...'

Virginia felt a little ashamed. You could take the girl out of the Counties... And looking at her father's diminished frame after 40 years of hard work, she felt like a thankless bitch. Clearly Stephen O'Reilly was helping two old and alone people to maintain a garden that was too incredibly large for them.

'Yes, I'm terrible, pappa,' she smiled at him. 'It's the bloody jetlag. Do you mind if I pop up for a quick nap?'

'Of course not, darling. I'll see Stephen has the boys back inside before supper's served... he knows your mother's rules and routines!'

She smiled and kissed him on her way out.

CHAPTER 41

Virginia wrapped her mother's cardigan about her and slipped out through the side door. Soft light spilled out from the kitchen window, across the damp grass. Her mother was washing dishes, her mouth moving non-stop, while her husband wiped a slow towel, across the plates, looking lost in thought.

Virginia sighed, lighting up her cigarette, instinctively sheltering the orange glow in case her mother spotted it. Of course she knew her mother was talking about her. About her divorce, about her accent, about the boys without a father, about her living halfway around the world... She could see it in the almost imperceptible tick at the deep line on the right side of her mother's mouth.

She would never please her mother; she'd realised that a long time ago. But, still, every time she saw that crease of disappointment, dragging her mother's mouth downward, she felt a stab of pain. Guilt. She blew out a cloud of smoke.

'Ah,' said Stephen, stretching back on the old wooden bench. 'So you *are* your father's daughter, then!'

She jumped back, startled, ground the half-smoked cigarette into the grass, and laughed nervously. 'What do you mean? What are you doing here, it's late...'

'Sorry, I didn't mean to startle you...'

'Yes you did, and I've wasted my last bloody cigarette.'

'Alright, I did. But forgive me; there's nothing quite like a daughter hiding her habits from her parents. At any age.'

'It's not a habit, and I'll thank you not bring age into this...' She smiled. 'But really, what are you doing here?'

'Your dad's been having trouble with the pump in the pond – I changed the valve today, and I was just on my way back home, so thought I'd come by and check it was ok.'

'That's incredibly kind of you, Stephen - '

'No! Not at all. Your parents are great people. Decent people, dare I say. They were so kind to my father during his illness. God knows not many would have retained a gardener who couldn't remember what day of the week it was, let alone what season.'

He laughed quietly. 'So what are you doing sitting out here on your own?' He pulled a cigarette packet from his pocket and pointed it toward her with a shrug.

'Cheeky sod,' she smiled, taking a cigarette from the pack. 'Oh, I'm escaping my mother's disappointment... There's a reason I don't come home too often.'

He smiled and nodded. 'God, I remember my father's reaction when I took up Landscaping. "Posh word for gardening!" he used to shout at me. What do you need a University for, when you've got me doing it all bloody day!'

She laughed. 'Yes, it's like that. My mother believes the failure of my marriage is down to my work. Not my actual job – just the fact that I work. Honestly, I've told her so many times about Clive – my ex – and his absolute obsession with work. *That's* what destroyed my marriage. But will she listen? Crap she will. She still sends him birthday cards, hoping he'll forgive me!'

Stephen smiled. 'Well, I'll tell you one thing – you've done an amazing job with those boys. Great kids. And obviously smart.'

'Oh, thanks. Yes, they are. I'm sure they get that from their father. I give them the boring stuff: boundaries, discipline, regularity.'

'Ah, so you're mother's daughter, too, then?' He smiled, squeezing her hand gently. The kitchen light was switched off, and the garden became cold and damp without the yellow splash of light. 'I'd best be off, Virginia. It was great talking to you, but I've got an entire plan to draw up tonight before I sleep.'

'Oh, yes, don't worry – I'm pretty exhausted. Thanks, Stephen – for looking after my parents.'

'No thanks needed.' Virginia turned away, walking toward the house. 'Virginia? I wonder – would you like to have dinner before you go back? Just the local pub – they're kid-friendly... we could take your folks?'

'That sounds fun,' she said awkwardly. 'But let's leave my parents at home; my mother hasn't seen me with a pint of Guinness, yet!'

CHAPTER 42

Clive woke early the next morning. He'd slept fitfully, dreaming of Nic and the boys. How had he managed to make such a mess of things? He threw off the covers and told himself to focus on now: on Walter Feldmann and Palmer.

He dressed, went out to the lounge and drew back the curtains. The morning mist was rising off the mountains and a watery pink line announced the dawn.

Gustav appeared, dishevelled, still in his robe, pale, clutching a handful of printouts.

'Have you seen what he's done, Clive?' he stumbled. 'He's sold us out...'

'Gustav! For God's sake!' he caught the old man as he fell. 'Sophie! George! Help me!'

The doctor was called, and Gustav was tucked up firmly in his bed. Gustav had initially refused medications, but after some cajoling from Clive and Sophie, had agreed to a small tranquiliser. 'Something to calm you, Monsieur,' the doctor had almost smiled.

Clive sat in the old leather chair beside the bed. The lamplight was low.

'Clive?' Gustav reached out his hand.

'Yes, Gustav, I'm here.'

'Did you read the reports?'

'Yes. He's getting ready to do a merger. I know.'

'He can't. Clive, he can't....'

'Calm Gustav – your heart can't take this. Your lawyer called. He's looking at the paperwork. He's coming up later this afternoon. So, for the moment....'

'For God's sake, Clive! There is no moment.... we have no time!'

'Gustav. Listen to me. You'll have even less time if you don't calm down. Please.' He squeezed the older man's hand.

Gustav fell back into the pillows, exhausted, and fell into a deep sleep.

Clive crept from the room.

'Sophie?' He found her arranging the sitting room. The dogs looked up hopefully as he entered, but fell back into depression when they saw it was not their master. 'I need to use Monsieur's computer and the phone – his secretary, Madame.....?'

'Madame Sylvian. Yes. She's based in Geneva – at the bank. She should arrive any moment.'

'Excellent. And can you confirm with M. Rocher that he is with us this afternoon. I need to know how far Walter can take this, in legal terms.'

'Of course. I'll call him immediately.'

Clive sat at the large wooden desk and began reading through the accounts Gustav had printed out overnight. The numbers looked like Japanese to him – he had never been good at numbers or maths. But now was not the time to admit defeat. He thought of Gustav. He thought of Gustav's father, and the boy he'd lost. He thought of Lilliana. No. Now was not the time to walk away.

He logged into his work email. Another message from that girl in Sales. Deborah. *I need to talk to you – please call me on my mobile.* And she gave the number. I'll call her later, he thought. One from James McKinnie's assistant. It seemed that Clive had been moved off the Feldmann's account, and that Palmer expected him back in London immediately. 'Fuck you!' Clive shouted, banging his fist down onto the table. He fell back into the chair. He'd have to tell Gustav. But not straight away. For the moment, he'd continue on as planned. Fuck James. Fuck Palmer. Fuck the job. Palmer and Walter were working together to screw Gustav, and if it was the last thing he did, Clive would stop them.

Madame Sylvian arrived after lunch. At 14h00. Precisely. She was a handsome woman, Clive thought. She was in her late fifties, early sixties. Dressed in an immaculate slate grey trouser suit, crease-free even after the drive, and a fuschia, silk blouse alluding to a sensuality and a touch of wildness. Gustav had complete trust in this woman; he'd employed her over 30 years ago, and had not been without her since.

She passed her coat to Sophie, and asked for her usual herbal tea.

'Yes, Madame,' Sophie said, her voice a little cool. 'I hope your vacance was restful?'

'Yes, thank you, Sophie. It was delightful. I shall take my tea with Monsieur Feldmann and then – '

'Madame – ' Clive stepped forward. 'Monsieur Feldmann is unavailable. I am Clive Alwynn and we'll be working together this afternoon. Sophie, we'll take our tea here...' Sophie nodded slightly and left the room.

He felt the full force of Mme Sylvian's glare behind her dark-rimmed glasses. 'Monsieur.' She nodded sharply, and shook Clive's outstretched hand. 'I know that Monsieur Feldmann has requested I work with you today, but I shall see him and then...'

'No, Madame. Please.... take a seat,' he gestured to the smaller table to the right of Gustav's desk. 'Gustav is gravely ill – ' she gasped, but he hurried on. 'His doctors have been with him. We have little time, Madame. Walter Feldmann has called an emergency Board meeting – tomorrow. At the bank. We have much work to do before then.'

'My God, but.... Gustav? Will he....'

'I don't know. But I do know he needs our help now. He assured me that you knew more about the running of the bank than he did.....' He ventured a smile.

'That is not true, Monsieur. But he did tell me he had every faith in you.... I trust you will not disappoint him?'

'No. I'll do my best – and, please, call me Clive. For the sake of transparency, I must tell you that I am no longer employed by AdVerbe - I am here only as a .... friend .... to Gustav.'

'Yes. We imagined that would happen once Walter had recruited Mr Palmer. Walter is very adept at recruiting accomplices. Where would you like me to begin?'

'Thank you,' he smiled gently. 'Perhaps we should start by looking at these', he gestured to the accounts printouts. 'The bank's central systems people called Gustav yesterday – there are large amounts of money being moved around. I can't make head or tail of the code they use.'

'Ah, yes,' Mme Sylvian peered at the sheets. 'These are the account codes for the bank itself. Not the clients' accounts – the business accounts for the bank... yes! These are very large amounts.'

'We need to know where they're being moved to? Other internal accounts? Or somewhere else entirely? I've been trying to call all of the Board members. See if we can find out anything else – or at least find out how many of them will back Walter – we need to buy some time.'

Clive dialled another number.

'Hello, may I speak to Michel Fallais? No. That's fine. I'll hold – no. I really do need to speak to Monsieur Fallais today. Yes – I understand. Thank you. I'll hold...' Then the secretary hung up on him. 'Damn it!' he shouted. 'Excuse me, Mme Sylvian, but these bloody people... they would try the patience of a saint.'

'And they often have,' she smiled. 'Do not worry, Clive. Pass me the phone, if you please.'

She pressed redial. 'Allo? Daphne? Oui! C'est Justine. Oui!' She put the call through to the speakerphone. 'Daphne? I was wondering... I am chez Monsieur Feldmann with Monsieur Alwynn... we desperately need to speak to Monsieur Fallais this afternoon.... '

'Oh? Well, I did not understand that this Englishman was working with you both! The other Englishman ... Palmer? He has told us all that this Alwynn has been removed from the Feldmann's account? And we were told that Monsieur Gustav was *trop malade* to be dealing with work matters...'

Justine Sylvian smiled at Clive's grimace.

'I'm sorry, Daphne, yes... Monsieur Alwynn is still working with us, perhaps Monsieur Palmer has been confused? Monsieur Gustav has been unwell, but today he is very much his normal self, I'm afraid...'

Daphne laughed conspiratorially.

'...and he is not so happy about this meeting being called so suddenly. Can you help me? He needs to see the dossiers which AdVerbe has distributed for the meeting – you know what Monsieur Gustav is like... he has 'lost' all of last week's emails!'

Daphne giggled. 'Yes, well, I have never heard of so much activity around an advertising! You see what happens when you have a few days away, Justine!'

'Precisely,' smiled Mme. Sylvian. 'May I rely on you?'

'Yes, of course, my friend! The files are on their way!'

Clive left her to it, nodding his appreciation; they both knew it was about much more than an 'advertising'. He wandered down to the kitchen where Sophie was busily preparing the evening meal.

'Ah, Clive! Will Mme Sylvian be joining us this evening?'

'No, she has a family dinner in Geneva...'

'Oh. Shame,' she sighed with little conviction.

Clive smiled, bending down to sniff gently at the casserole.

'God, Sophie! That smells divine!'

She blushed. 'Thank you, Clive. Will you be ready for this meeting? I am worried that Walter will try and stop you from attending...'

'He's already told Mme. Sylvian she won't be needed.... I'm sure he'll try something – but it really doesn't matter if we actually attend the meeting or not.'

'What? I thought you were going to explain to the Board that Walter's plans were wrong – I thought you were going to stop him!' She banged down the spoon.

'It's ok, Sophie.' He touched her shoulder gently. 'Everything is going to be fine. How is Gustav? Was that the doctor's car I saw earlier?'

'Yes. George is with him now – perhaps you should visit with him before dinner?' and she wiped away a tear.

He reached over and kissed her gently on the forehead. 'Sophie – everything will be alright.'

'Yes, well…. Clive? Have you spoken to your wife? I see that Madame Sylvian has been using the phone all day…'

'Yes,' he lied. 'I've left her a message… she's very busy at the moment. I expect she'll call later.'

He needed to call Deborah and see what had happened at that meeting this morning.

CHAPTER 43

Nicole rested her hand on the rusty, cold metal of the ornate gate. She looked up to the square, unrelenting outline of the church shouldering against the sodden hills and the grey clouds illuminated by the occasional flash of lightning.

'*Where are you, Elizabeth*?' she whispered. Emily Previs had shown her the black-bordered card just before she left the house: '*Elizabeth Parnell: We ask you to say a prayer for our lost sister. St James's Church. Sunday, December 11, 1768.*' Of course, Elizabeth's stone would be long lost to the Northern weather and moss; Nicole winced as another gust of wind seemed to tear the top branches from the old trees.

You can never be lost.
I told you: each footfall
I hear: a broken branch; a sigh; a surprised smile;
The echoes of the empty waiting hours.
Don't you see?
I was waiting for you even before you were lost.

'Lost,' she laughed bitterly. She pulled her coat about her, and slapped at the torch, willing the batteries to life. It was nearly dark. Dark December like the day they'd buried Elizabeth Parnell. She shuddered as a low rumble of thunder made the ground shudder. 'Damn it!' she said. 'Get a grip, woman!'

'This is useless,' she sighed as she walked toward the church. The stained glass windows were illuminated by a low, electric candle light. Of course, the door was locked. The wind seemed to be dropping away, or perhaps that's what she hoped. She wondered, half-heartedly, if she shouldn't come back tomorrow, but she knew she wouldn't sleep until she'd found Elizabeth.

Clearly, the gravestones in the front of the church were too recent. She climbed the slope to the side of the church and followed the gravel path, running her hand along the skeleton creepers and ivy forging their way through the emerging moss, soft and spongy in the trickle of the leaking pipes.

The hillside above her was littered with stones and monuments leaning wildly to the right and left. The apple trees from the neighbouring field lay their failing, full weight on the crumbling churchyard wall, shading a row of small nondescript stones that had sunken into the long grass.

A crack of lighting and the clouds seemed to burst overhead, the rain thundering against the roof of the church. Nicole slapped the torch again. She dropped her bag by the wall and knelt down to read the washed away names and dates. No messages of loss, no poetry. These were the stones of the poor and the disowned.

The yellow torch beam brushed across the next stone. Nicole ran her fingers along the shallow letters, scraping a little against the yellow-orange lichen: '...eth Parne..' then '17..' then 'Josh...'. She fell against the stone and stretched her hand across it.

She had found Elizabeth and her son.

Back in the car, she wiped away the rain and unfolded Elizabeth's last letter:

'My dearest, by this time next week, I believe our child will have arrived. I want to say 'son', but of course, only God knows what blessing is coming to us. Please, my love, should God take me sooner, I know you will hold this child close, knowing our hearts – we three – are one.'

Nicole fell forward against the steering wheel, recalling the police record of Elizabeth's death:

The woman, Elizabeth Parnell, was found, dressed in a white gown, in her bed. Her infant son was bound and swaddled at her side.

Both had been cleaned and prepared, and we ascertain that a midwife was present. Lamps were burning low, indicating the child had been born in the early evening.

The woman was not married, and her Father, Edward Parnell has declared no interest or liability with regard to the deceased. Arrangements for the burial have been passed to the Parish and Reverend Rosswell.

CHAPTER 44

Stephen laughed at Jack's frown. 'You poor lad! You don't know what a *Scampi* is?'

Jack's frown deepened. 'No.' And he looked to his mother for reassurance, but she raised the menu to cover her smile.

'A Scampi,' said Stephen earnestly, 'is a creature that lives in the river near here. You won't be getting any of *that* in your New York.'

'Is it a fish?' asked Ben.

'Is it a fish!' Stephen laughed a little, and added a theatrical shudder. '*Is it a fish*, he asks...you'd wish it was if you ever ran into one.'

'Well, what is it?' asked Jack, feigning disinterest.

'Well now... I've never seen one – well not one in the wild. But I've seen the poor men who catch them. Every week they come in from their boats... but they look very different from the poor men who went out...'

'Why?' Ben's eyes grew wider. 'What happens to them?'

Stephen sighed, and took a sip of wine. 'The Scampi. It gets them – well, not all of them....'

Jack was starting to look nervous. 'What do you mean 'it gets them'?'

Virginia lowered the menu and frowned warningly: 'Yes, what do you mean 'it gets them' considering I want to sleep tonight?'

'Oh, well,' Stephen picked up his menu. 'I didn't realise you yanks were so easily scared. Maybe I should just leave it now...'

'No!' Jack almost shouted.

'Well, let's talk about The Scampi, then....'

By the time the main course plates were cleared, Jack and Ben were exhausted, laughing noiselessly, flush-cheeked and holding their ribs. By the time dessert arrived, Ben had fallen sideways into Jack's lap, and Jack struggled to keep his eyes open.

'You're amazing!' Virginia smiled at Stephen. 'I haven't seen them *so* happy in *so* long...'

'Are they not happy in the States?'

'Oh, of course... it's just that...'

'Virginia...' he reached out and placed his hand over hers. 'Virginia, I wasn't having a go. It's just that these two were meant to laugh and if they haven't been, then...'

She sighed. 'You're right. They were meant to laugh. It's just that since the divorce – ' she looked quickly to Jack, who was only half asleep. 'Look, we should get them back. Do you mind if we settle up?'

When they got back to the house, Virginia saw the lounge curtains twitching. 'Oh, God. My mother. She's appalling. Anyone would think I was 16!'

Stephen laughed as he lifted Jack over his shoulder. 'No, it's just the reputation of the Irish gardener that's frightening them…'

CHAPTER 45

Robert was late; Polly rearranged the table setting again, watching Clive pace the lounge, picking up a framed photo here and there, then looking at his watch.

'Yes Clive, he's late,' she smiled. 'He often is. I suspect that you rarely are...'

He nodded. 'Rarely.'

'Don't think it's not important to him – '

'I know,' and his attempt at a smile failed miserably.

She blushed slightly. 'I'm just so damned nervous – so is he.'

'And I'm not?'

She went to the kitchen and he looked again at the pictures of Robert's children – his brother and sister. He ran a hand through his hair.

The front door opened and a huge gust of wind seemed to clear the room of his thoughts.

Robert stepped down the first, then the second step. He slowly unwound his scarf, twice, and put his bag down beside him. Clive stepped forward, but then back. Robert shook his coat out and draped it onto the bannister. Clive looked across to Polly as she hurried into the room.

'Robert. Darling. Come in,' and she hurried forward and tried to take his arm.

He pushed her away gently. 'It's alright Poll.' He stood to his full height, his chin slightly up and forward. 'You must be Clive,' and his voice seemed to catch a little on itself.

Clive stepped forward, reached out his hand; his father seemed to stumble on the last step and they grabbed at one another. 'Robert,' he said, surprised at the emotion that was overwhelming him.

Polly watched from the lounge. In the stillness of the moment she felt she could not move; could not walk or speak.

'Sorry I'm late,' Robert said as he ushered Clive toward the couch. 'Traffic. Business. You know how it is.'

'Yes. I do.'

'You found us alright, then?'

'Yes. Polly gives good directions.'

They both nodded toward her, and she smiled. 'Robert, darling, you'd like a drink?' He nodded quickly and she hurried to the kitchen.

'She's a good woman,' Robert sighed.

'She is,' said Clive. 'Look… Robert…'

They spoke at the same time: 'Clive, look, I …'

Clive smiled. 'Robert. I don't know why we're here. I mean, I don't know what you're expecting from me.'

'I know. It's awkward. I think Poll thought she was doing the right thing...'

'You mean ... you didn't organise this?'

Robert coughed. 'No!' And then more gently: 'Bloody woman gets these ideas into her head all the time!'

'Right,' Clive smiled sarcastically. 'Well, let's just get through this evening and I'll be out of your way, then.'

Robert looked angry suddenly. 'No! That's not what I meant, I just meant that...' Polly sensed the atmosphere as she walked in. 'Robert! Clive!' She felt small and insignificant between the two of them. 'Sit down! Please...'

The doorbell rang.

Jocelyn shouted at Jamie to 'bring the babies' things!' and slammed the front door behind her. There was a pause while she composed herself in the hall mirror, then she hurried down the stairs.

Robert was already standing to greet her, Polly sat back a little in her chair and took a long sip of her champagne. Clive took a deep breath, and watched her negotiate her way down the stairs.

'Daddy!' Jocelyn threw her heavy self around her father. 'How are you?' And she kissed him on the forehead. 'Polly! Mmmahhh!' and she blew a kiss toward her. 'Oh! And you must be *Clive*!'

Clive looked up at his half-sister – realising that she, like him, was looking for some sort of resemblance in the other. She was much heavier than him. She had her father's double chins, and her waist and belly had thickened with the burden of three pregnancies. Her hair was dark and wild and despite the obvious signs of sprays or gels to calm it. He stood up awkwardly and reached out his hand.

'Oh Clive,' she fluttered. 'No need for such formality! We are *family* after all!' She lunged forward to kiss him firmly on both cheeks.

'Jocelyn,' he smiled uneasily.

The front door blew open and Jamie fell into the hall, two toddlers at his heel and one perched on his hip. 'Hello all!' he shouted, the overloaded bag sliding from his shoulder, toys and baby bottles scattering on the floor.

Robert hurried forward to rescue the bag. 'Hello Jamie. Come meet your brother-in-law!'

Jamie smiled warmly. 'Hi Clive. It's a pleasure...'

'Jamie!' Jocelyn barked from the table. 'For goodness sake! Where's Tristan?'

'He was just here...' Jamie looked around his ankles anxiously.

'Don't worry, Jocelyn. He's here!' Polly pulled the giggling boy from under the table. 'And he's coming with Poll to the kitchen, aren't you darling?' She smothered his face with little kisses. 'Jamie, sit down. I'll take Tamsin ... Robert, will you pour Jamie a drink. God knows he looks like he needs it!'

'Don't we all...' Justin came in from the kitchen. 'Back door was unlocked Poll. You should be careful... never know who might slip in.'

Clive turned and was surprised to see a softer, paler version of himself. Judging by the look on Justin's face, he'd also seen the resemblance. But it didn't please him.

CHAPTER 46

The Board members gathered around the table, their bones creaking and sighing as they fell into the plush leather chairs.

Walter waved away the staff and their coffee pots.

'Gentlemen... I am sorry to say that my brother, Gustav, will not be joining us today. He is seriously ill... I'm sure you'll join me in a short prayer for him?'

They bowed their heads and murmured their condolences.

'So,' Walter cleared his throat. 'To the business of the day. You will, perhaps, recognise Mr Palmer?' He gestured to his right. Palmer stood up and bowed slightly. 'Mr Palmer will now present our new advertising campaign, and after that we shall get down to the *real* business! You'll find today's agenda very exciting!' He gestured to a young secretary who passed a beautifully bound dossier to each member.

'Today, gentleman, we launch a new Feldmann's!'

The lights of the conference room dimmed, as the screen lit up. There was a stunned silence as the Board members made sense of what they were watching: a young, Asian girl, perhaps 12 or 13, pinned down by a group of older, Western men – one of whom was Walter Feldmann.

The assembled board members jaws seemed to drop toward the table in a silent unison. At that moment, Clive entered the room silently and took the DVD remote control from Palmer's hand. He pressed pause, just at the money shot.

'Gentlemen,' he spoke softly, gesturing to one of the leggy assistants to up the lights. 'I suggest you take a good look at the dossiers in front of you. They are the company records for a film company owned and run by Monsieur Walter Feldmann... Oh, no need to panic,' he smiled at the advancing security guard. 'I am here on behalf of Monsieur Gustav Feldmann – the Bank's Director General. He sends his regards.' And he handed Gustav's signed consent to the still shell-shocked Walter. 'I think, Gentlemen,' Clive continued, 'that we need to have a close look at the current situation – and the rather bizarre ideas that have been flying around lately... Monsieur Feldmann – Gustav Feldmann – is not happy with the current situation.'

The board members nodded vigorously, some making disgruntled sounds in Walter's direction.

No one, except Clive, noticed that Palmer had quietly slipped away.

'Excuse me for a moment, won't you. Perhaps this would be a good moment to top up our coffees... or maybe some of us need something stronger,' Clive said. 'Lisle?' he called to one of the blondes, standing speechless in the corner. 'Can you organise some more refreshments, please...'

He strode into the reception area, and saw Palmer frantically punching messages into his Blackberry, and barking orders at the receptionist. 'Did you hear me? I want a taxi to the airport. Now!' He caught sight of Clive and adjusted his false smile and loosened his tie, as if trying to get some colour into his ashen features.

'There's one for the records, hey Clive?' he laughed mirthlessly. 'Bloody old pervert. I'm just trying to get hold of James, he'll know what we should…'

Clive snatched the Blackberry from his sweating hands. 'You are – you always were – an obnoxious little shit, Palmer. You couldn't even pull this off, could you? How long have you been kissing Walter Feldmann's arse? I bet from the start. No need for you to email James; I did that about an hour ago – he needs to be ready for the fallout. AdVerbe working with pornographers and drug dealers… what *will* Paris think?'

Palmer tried to stand taller, tucking his crumpled shirt into the tight waistband of his trousers. 'Now look here, Clive… You can't just dismiss Walter, the Board is totally behind him. I think we…'

'Shut up,' Clive said quietly, scrolling through the Blackberry messages. 'Ah, yes. Here it is. A message from James. I imagine HR is copied in… probably best to read it on your way to the airport.' And he tossed the Blackberry back to Palmer.

Palmer's smile turned into a sneer. 'You bloody jumped-up piece of shit!' he spat. 'It'll take me five minutes to sort this crap out, and let me tell you something… it'll be your arse that takes the rap for this fuck-up. You just don't seem to understand… there's blokes like me, and there's blokes like you. Blokes like *you* never win, mate.'

The 'mate' was too much. Before Clive – or Palmer – knew what happened, Palmer was sprawled on the floor, the blonde receptionist squealing, blood pouring from his nose, and Clive stepped over him, stroking his bruised knuckles and returned to the boardroom.

CHAPTER 47

Stephen was in the kitchen when she came downstairs. 'Are they tucked in?'

'Yes,' she whispered. 'And even better, my mother's gone to bed, so we can probably risk a cigarette in the lounge.'

He smiled gently and moved toward her. 'Well that would be a brave move... '

She moved back a little further into the lounge. 'Maybe if we opened the doors to the garden?' She reached for the side lamps that her mother had turned off hours before. 'Honestly, I can't see a thing...'

He grabbed her hand and pulled her close to him. 'Virginia... come here...' and he kissed her deeply. 'Come on. Let's go.'

She was a little dizzy, and she pushed back her hair and laughed a little. 'Oh, Stephen, it's late, I...'

'Come on...' he was already in the kitchen. He closed the door firmly behind them.

'But what about the boys?'

He pushed her against the car and kissed her again. 'They're fine. Your mother's not really asleep. Come home with me.'

The drive to his house was surreal. She looked out of the window, turning away quickly from his profile – the strong jaw, the large, but not unattractive nose. He sometimes looked to her. They said nothing.

CHAPTER 48

Palmer went straight to the business class lounge at the airport. His flight was not for another few hours, but he needed a drink and he needed to figure out what to do next. James McKinnie's email had been pretty blunt: talk to HR, they've got all the details. Three drinks later, the pain of his bruised mouth was lessening.

'Drowning your sorrows, Alex?' Debs was perched on the stool beside him. She was dressed in a light grey business suit, her soft pink silk blouse opened lazily across the top of her breasts.

'D-Debs?' he stuttered with confusion. 'What are you doing here? Client meeting?'

'How was the board meeting? Here,' she signalled the waiter. 'Same again.'

'Oh, great...' he slurred. 'We did a great presso...' he looked at her breasts and then down to the high heels as she crossed her legs again.

'Really?' she smiled, adjusting his tie. 'Oh, Alex. You've got blood on your shirt. What happened?' And she touched his bruised mouth, gently.

He sighed. 'Oh, nothing... just a problem with Clive Alwynn again. But don't worry... we did really well. The bank loves us!' And he threw back his drink. 'This account is in the bag, alright. What time's your flight? Would you like another?' he nodded at her G&T.

'Yes, please. I have all the time in the world, Palmer,' and she stretched back, knowing her breasts were rising high in her push-up bra. 'You must feel so good – taking the helm of an account like Feldmann's? Do you think you can find a role for me on the team?'

Palmer took it all in. 'Yes,' he said in a low voice. 'We worked well together in the past, didn't we?'

She laughed softly. 'How did they enjoy the film, then?'

'Huh?' Palmer was confused.

'I did a little editing in my film course at Uni, but the technology today makes it so much easier... we wanted to get all the best bits into a very short time frame...'

He stared at her, uncomprehendingly. 'What are you talking about...? You mean you...?'

'Yes,' she stopped smiling and dabbed at her mouth with the cocktail serviette. 'I did it. I tracked down Walter's film. I made sure Clive Alwynn knew about it. I edited it and I put together all the financial background on Walter Feldmann - the dossiers the board are reading right now, I imagine. So spare me the bullshit.' She stood up to leave. 'Oh for God's sake, shut your mouth. You're nearly drooling. You're a fucking loser, Palmer. You always have been.'

'Debs, for fuck's sake....' he reached for her arm, and she pulled it away violently.

'Only yesterday afternoon', she continued, 'Marina was showing me the numbers you'd submitted to Paris. I told her they were way out. Tsk, tsk, Alex! What on earth were you thinking?'

He seemed to be gasping for air.

'Oh, but don't worry. I've promised Clive I'll go through it all with a fine tooth comb,' she smiled at him as he seemed to collapse under the weight of every word. 'Didn't I tell you? *I'm* taking over Feldmann's – only interim, of course – just until Clive comes back. I'm chuffed, actually: it was Clive's idea! I don't know how you got away with it all these years.

Probably because you had your head up James McKinnie's arse. Well, that won't help you anymore. You're both gone.'

Palmer stumbled up from his stool.

'Oh, yes.... didn't I mention? It seems your fiddling the books was the distraction McKinnie needed to do his own fiddling...seems he'd built his own little 'Super User' account. It's serious shit, Alex. The Gendarmes are on it.

I've got to go, but there's no reason you wouldn't stay on a little longer. Barman? One more here... and he'll take the bill. Thanks, Alex. It's been fun.'

And with that, she sashayed out of the bar wheeling her overnight bag behind her.

CHAPTER 49

James McKinnie sighed. The Paris office had left 20 messages with his secretary. 'Amy?' he buzzed for her. 'Amy? What do they want?'

He and Paolo had been at lunch, then spent the afternoon shopping. He was flushed and a little drunk. He was, he thought, getting a little old for this... getting too old for Paris, and maybe getting too old for Paolo. He clutched at the sales receipts spilling from his jacket pocket. Honestly, how many cashmere sweaters did one man need? And then there were the shoes... my God! And the tantrums, the tears... The cost of Paolo's love had risen every year, until now, James found himself unable to pay. Despite the bonuses, despite 'juggling' finances, Paolo's insatiable appetite remained so.

James had imagined a relaxed, moderately long, retirement. A yacht moored near Antibes, waking late, swimming, slipping into shore for a long lunch, back to the yacht for an afternoon of indulgence with Paolo, and then a DVD or a game of cards before bed. But Paolo would never be quiet; could never be calm.

Amy's high-pitched voice came over the intercom: 'James, Marina and....'

The office door opened.

It was Marina Merriland and Robert Dwyer, the head of Human Resources.

'What is it?' James said trying to compose himself.

'James,' Robert said. 'We need to talk...'

'Really, Robert,' James tapped wildly at his computer keyboard. 'This will have to wait...we've got the Feldmann's account and I ....'

'It will wait,' said Robert. 'Paris has asked Marina and I to freeze your access to our systems.'

James swallowed hard. 'Honestly, bloody French cloak and dagger. Marina, can't we do it later? I know Feldman's looks dodgy, but I'm talking to Palmer and I think we can...'

'No, I really must insist James. Do you mind stepping away from the machine.' Robert moved forward and James saw the security guard through the open door. 'I've been instructed to escort you from the building – no, please leave the phone and the Blackberry.'

As the elevator doors opened into the pristine lobby, the detectives cuffed McKinnie and led him to the waiting car. 'Call my lawyer!' he bellowed to the receptionist.

CHAPTER 50

Robert Jeffreys tried to reach his hand across the cold linen; he was so cold. Last night, the sheets had been damp and clinging; hot, yet cold. He heard the foxes - too close to the house; it was March and they were screeching and scratching for one another somewhere down the garden. He wondered if he'd added that to his List for Poll: she had to ask Mr Warley to shoot them. He laughed silently, knowing she never could.

He wanted to reach out to her now, but his arm was leaden. She sighed and turned in her sleep, reaching back to him with a gentle caress. *Poll!* He wanted to cry out. *Poll!* But his throat was twisted into the final stages of his illness.

He fell into a deep sleep and watched his dreams; they unwound like a film. '*That's what they mean,*' he thought. *You see your life flash before you...*' He watched the colours, he touched hands, he felt the fabric of his uncle's coat... it was all so real. He heard Poll. Why was she crying? *Poll?* It wasn't cold anymore. And here was Clive. His son. His *other* son. He watched his face; he watched its furrows, he felt he knew the deeper lines around the eyes, the mouth.

The air was dry and everything was coloured in blues... And there was Poll.

'*Babe,*' she said. '*It's ok to go now. It's ok to go... I love you.*'

He felt his fingertips against the sheets; the weave of the cotton. He could smell flowers; maybe it was Poll's perfume, maybe it was the skin at her throat. The film ran again. It was late Summer and the sun was flooding, low, through the trees; a last blaze of soft orange, black at the edges.

And Poll was singing again. *Flaming September, what can you show me that is real?* And he worried for her.

He wanted to cry out: '*Clive? Clive'*

Clive Alwynn reached down and kissed his father's forehead. *'It's alright,'* he said. *'I'll look after her.'*

Robert Jeffreys tried to reach up through the heavy air, and was surprised when his wasted, skeletal hands sank into the warm grasp of his son and his wife.

He sighed as the pictures faded, and there were words on the air: *Godspeed. Safe. Love. Forever. Time. Leave.* And the foxes screeched into the empty night.

CHAPTER 51

Michael instructed the Concierge to hold all calls. 'Please, can you just say that I've checked out already?'

'Of course, Sir. And your wife? Shall we also say…?'

'Of course not!' Michael snapped. 'I'm sorry, no, of course, put my wife through straight away.'

He turned away, then stopped dead. 'Nicola?'

She was sunk deep in a leather chair. She looked pale and distracted her still-damp hair had fallen loose from its clasp.

Michael noticed the Concierge's eager interest. 'Nicola – come up to my room. We can talk…'

'Your wife?' she hissed, still not moving.

'Please, Nicola. This is not the place.'

She stood up slowly and walked toward the elevator.

'Whiskey?' he asked, as he closed the door to his room.

She looked out across the darkening sky.

'When were you going to mention it, Michael?'

'I wanted to – I need to …'

'When the fuck were you going to tell me that you'd married your student!'

'It's not like that.' He looked away.

'Oh no? What's it like? Come on, Michael! You're the one looking for closure.'

He swallowed another mouthful of whiskey. 'Yes. Charlotte and I married.'

'When?'

He waited a long time before answering. 'About a month after you left.'

She stared at him blankly, uncomprehendingly.

'One month?'

He stammered. 'We ... I had to ...'

'Oh my god ...' She covered her mouth and ran to the bathroom to vomit. She rinsed her face with cold water, and stood in the doorway, watching him fold into a chair, his face in his hands.

'She was pregnant, wasn't she?'

He nodded.

She picked up her coat and bag.

'Nicola, look – I had to! For god's sake – she refused to get rid of it and she threatened to tell everyone – the college, you ...'

'How long had it been going on, Michael?'

He bowed his head a little. 'About six months.'

She ignored his calls as she slammed the door behind her. So, she and Charlotte had been pregnant at the same time. But Charlotte had stood her ground and demanded he take responsibility; she was too young to know that Michael was too self-absorbed to become a husband, a father. Look! Even now, here he was in London visiting Nicole behind his wife's back!

'How far gone was she?' she'd asked.

'Three months,' he'd said. 'But Nic. If you would have stayed – we could have faced that together. We would have gotten through it – I never would have left you. I loved you.'

'Oh, for Fuck's sake, Michael!' the rage seemed to erupt from her. 'Will this never end? You wanted closure, I gave you closure. The end. I did not love you Michael. And I don't love you now. We used each other. That's all it was. I needed security, god knows I probably needed a bloody father figure. You needed another undergraduate to impress. And now, you need some kind of fantasy, some kind of get-out clause. Charlotte was the get-out clause when you were with me – I'm not going to be your get-out now you're with her.'

He turned away, but she continued on.

'You know that panic you told me about? That feeling of drowning? It's not about wanting *me*; it's not about *wanting* at all! It's about *not wanting*.... not wanting the life you've made for yourself. Well, I'm sorry Michael. That's the life you got.'

It all seemed so true – but back at the house, she wondered about Charlotte and her courage in keeping the baby. Sure, Michael had been pathetic. He'd been a self-indulgent coward. But hadn't she been just as pathetic? Just as self-indulgent? If she'd really wanted to keep Michael Forester's baby – her baby – nothing would have stopped her.
The truth was that she had not wanted to have a baby, and she had taken the necessary steps. There was no one else to blame. She curled up under the blankets and embraced the cold, grey day.

CHAPTER 52

Nicole smiled, hearing William Hartnett's hesitant knock at the front door. Bella seemed to sense the hesitancy, too, barking gently, her head turned to one side in confusion.

'William!' Nicole smiled and hugged him. 'I'm so glad you could come.'

'I don't think I could have missed this for the world,' he smiled. 'Oh, I see you've got a dog,' he laughed, as Bella jumped against him.

'Bella! Get down! Come in… if you take your bag up – I've put you in the boys' room. Second on the right. Bathroom's to the left. Glass of red?' she called from the kitchen.

'Yes, please.' William switched on the light. It was a beautiful room. Two single beds; a simple chest of drawers in a pale pine. The window was almost floor to ceiling, a heavy white curtain half tied back, accenting the darkening sky, all slate grey with watery streaks of pink. Books lined one wall – an atlas, a dictionary, an encyclopedia of sport. On the other, a collage of family snaps: two blonde smiling boys tumbling in and out of the frame, their father (he assumed this was Clive) holding them, laughing with them, throwing their small bodies into the air in a freeze-framed moment of joy. And there, to one side, Nicole and the dog and the boys dancing a mad whirl on top of a hill – the sky behind them filled with agitated, flashing kites, their hair all around them and across their faces, all three laughing and breathless in the cold day.

Downstairs, Nicole turned to greet him. 'How was your trip down?' And she handed him a glass.

'Oh great. I love trains...' he laughed quietly. 'Those pictures in the room... they're great. It's a great collage...'

'Oh...yeah. I've just redecorated the room. The boys – Clive's sons will be coming over in the Summer. I wanted it to be nice for them – some memories. There's a cupboard under the stairs. I gave it a big clean out and found this box file full of photos...'

'They look like nice kids.'

'They are... they're gorgeous. Anyway – come through into the lounge. Do you mind eating later?'

'No, I ate on the train... so what's this 'surprise' you had for me?'

She smiled, gesturing for him to sit on the sofa. 'Well, don't be too expectant! It's just that when you emailed me to say you were down here for a conference, anyway, I thought you might like to drop by and see the proposal for Elizabeth's book. Well, my book *about* Elizabeth.' She handed him a small, bound manuscript of about 50 pages.

'Oh God,' he looked overwhelmed. 'I'm honoured...'

'Oh, don't get carried away!' she laughed nervously. 'I'm not sure I've done her justice...'

'I'm sure you have,' he said, scanning the first page. 'But Nicole? Tell me the story – read it to me, or just tell it to me. I'd love to hear it from you... I mean, you found her...'

She smiled. 'OK. Let me top up that wine glass first... Right. You know the first half – her father packed her off to the States to marry his best friend's son.'

'Yes. But she came back...did she hate America so much? Or was it the bloke?'

'Her letters – the ones I found in Emily's barn – they tell us she loved America. The space, the air, the freedom... Listen to this...it's a letter to her mother... At this stage she's living with her future sister-in-law...' she flipped through the pages.

To wake on a clear morning, knowing that in minutes the heat will take your breath away and this silence – this brief, cool moment just before the first sliver of sun rises above the horizon – will be a very different silence: the silence of heat and slow-flying bugs and trees almost fanning themselves in an effort to make a breeze. And then, just after noon, we ride the horses – no saddle, no frippery – to the lake. We tie the horses and undress – down to nothing! (I hope you are not too shocked!) – and dive into the nearly cool water. We stay there, laughing and playing until evening. Then we go home and there's sure to be some amusement: a dinner, a dance, visiting the cousins... watching the vast yellow fields, the soft purple glow of evening creeping across them. And the insects singing in rhythm.

'She loved it,' sighed Nicole.

'Then what happened? Why did she come back?'

'Ahhh... right. That letter was to her mother, right? Well, she wrote quite a few more to Thomas – the schoolmaster.'

'Her married lover?'

'Yes. They'd made a plan. She'd go out to the States… she'd turn down her betrothed, but stay in America. Thomas was going to leave his wife and join Elizabeth there. The plan was to disappear, start again … but he never came for her. The letters stopped.'

'So, she married the American guy?' he asked, frowning. 'But she died here?'

Nicole sighed. 'She came back for him. She told her fiance's family about the plan and they gladly paid for her journey home. Can you imagine how disgraced she was at that stage?'

'And what happened? Did he realise how much she loved him? Did he leave his wife?'

'No. He didn't leave his wife - he couldn't - it was just too scandalous.'

'But she had his baby?'

'The baby only lived for a couple of hours - he died an hour after she did.'

'My God… what a bastard he was!'

'He wasn't brave enough - but her heart was. She knew he couldn't honour what they had - no matter how hard she tried.'

CHAPTER 53

Sophie Géroux folded the sheets carefully around Gustav Feldmann's shoulders. She'd opened the windows a little way this morning – the air seemed so stale after the weeks of waiting. The doctor had been and gone hours ago; now they waited for the undertaker.

She went to the cupboard and took out the blue suit Monsieur Feldmann had been married in.

She touched Clive's shoulder – gently. He started up from the chair.

'Clive. It is morning. He is gone.'

Clive blinked a couple of times.

'Right. Yes – thank you, Sophie.'

He sighed. Gustav Feldmann looked at peace. Isn't that what they always said of the dead? But, certainly, this was a man with no more worries. For a brief moment, Clive envied him. But – no. He drew back the curtains and watched the day opening up before him; a round rose-coloured sun lifted slowly upwards between the slate-grey hillsides.

He'd arrived late last night and spent the early morning with Gustav. The morphine had made the old man comfortable and, perhaps, a little lucid. He'd talked of Lilliana and the dogs, his brothers, the open-topped cars, the parties.

And he spoke to his son, Thierry, imagining he saw the boy there. 'You must remember, my boy: we are reaching for you, still. The water is deep, but we are still reaching for you. Give me your hand! Do not be angry! We did not want to let you go... reach out for me!'

Clive had fallen into a deep sleep, in the chair at Gustav's bedside. He'd dreamt of Nic and the boys – Bella dancing about, blown about by the wind. Sebastian winding chains of figure-eights between his ankles. He reached out.

He placed a warm hand on Gustav's pale cheek. The dogs looked up – expectantly, needing direction.

'Allez!' He opened the patio doors and the dogs ran into the watery warmth of the morning sun.

* * * *

The undertaker had departed. Sophie Géroux leant against Clive's arm as her husband closed the wrought iron gates.

'You will join us for supper, Clive?'

'I will – I need to speak with George. Gustav asked me to see to a few of his personal effects – the photo albums...'

'Yes. The solicitor told us you would access to his files. And you're staying for the funeral, I'm sure....'

'Yes – I won't be too much trouble, I hope.'

'Clive,' she shook her head. 'We are honoured... you gave him much comfort . . .'

A car crawled up the drive, and, after speaking with the driver, George opened the gates to let it through. The dogs, quiet for the afternoon, gave a low growl. Clive recognised the way she moved as she stepped from the car, her silhouette familiar and wonderful.

George took the small bag she carried and Nicole walked up the drive, the sound of the gravel beneath her shoes.

Sophie looked to Clive, and seeing the joy and love in his expression, she turned toward the house.

Clive reached out his hand to his wife, and she fell against him, burying her face at his neck.

'Come inside,' he whispered.